Changing Forever

And

Other Stories

By

Bill Griffin

First printing 2019

ISBN

978-1-9993523-3-2

Seanchai Publishing

Ballinahallia

Moycullen

Co.Galway

Ireland H91 CXE0

Griffin1354@yahoo.co.uk

I have tried to recreate events, locales and conversations from my memories of them. In order to maintain their anonymity in some instances I have changed the names of individuals and places. I may have changed some identifying characteristics and details such as physical properties, occupations and places of residence.

Contents

An Ordinary Murder

The murderer lived six doors up in the same small street as Billy. Of course he hadn't always been a murderer. It's not something you are born to or have to serve your time at. It occurs in one defining moment that binds two lives in a tragic duality. And when the victim is a thirteen year old girl then the transformation of one to angel and the other to demon continues the oldest, understood duality in the world and one especially understood in a small Irish village as yet untouched by the hedonism of the sixties.

The house he lived in stood out in the street. The walls bore evidence that the convention of a new coat of whitewash before the annual Corpus Christi procession in May had been ignored for many a year. The flaking patchwork of off whites and washed out yellows were exposed by the rain showers regularly whipping down from the mountains, over the bridge and up the narrow street. White paint curled on the grimy window frames exposing their wood to the elements. Streaked window panes bounced sunlight onto the cracked footpath, offering little insight to passers-by of the interior.

It's decline had started the day Joey Farrell's mother, a widow of less than three years, failed to turn up at the corner shop at half past nine for her few messages. She couldn't afford the financial risk of shopping weekly. One of the girls in the shop called down and found her on the kitchen floor, tea towel still grasped in her hand, her wraparound apron still damp having succumbed to the familial trait of weak and often broken hearts. Joey was an orphan three months after making his First Holy Communion. The curtains were drawn by a neighbour as his mother was taken from the hospital mortuary to the church and Joey was taken by the 'authorities' to a home in the county town of Clonmel.

Six months later he returned in the company of a small man whom Joey said was his uncle who had spent years in England. The man, when he cared to, introduced himself as Robert P Farrell. His soft hands seemed to confirm his story that he had worked in insurance in London for many years.

As neither Joey's mother nor father was from one of the long established families in the area his story could not be checked out. As his clipped English accent became intermingled with the soft burr of the Tipperary brogue his name was shortened, in the time honoured fashion of communities familiar with themselves, to Robert P. For years Billy and his friends who only knew him by that name used to giggle out of earshot about having the surname Pee. The curtains were drawn back allowing light to penetrate the dark cornered rooms and the accumulated dust was allowed to gradually fall to the floor with each pulling. The electricity that buzzed on the wires along the street remained at the tarred pole outside the front room window. It was Robert P's contention that the state should give the supply free to those on the Social. For a man who had supposedly spent years in gainful employment he seemed well versed in Social welfare systems of his former and current homelands.

The doubts about him grew when he refused offers of work in the forestry and with local farmers who employed most of the available male workforce in the village of four hundred odd souls. Joey's mother's death caught all her friends by surprise as they were still dealing with the death of her big quiet husband from the unmentionable big C. But as they became more familiar with Joey's new guardian the daily parade of aproned women bringing two hot plates to the house slowed and finally stopped.

In the snug of the local pub cum shop sympathy for that 'poor crathur of a boy' drained with the drops of sherry taken by the women who wouldn't be 'caught dead' going into a pub without their husbands. Comments flew up and down the one long seat that filled the snug opposite the sliding wooden hatch that separated the pub in body and mind from these respectable women.

"It's not right you know; a young fellow like that being brought up in a house with no woman."

"You're right, girl, it wouldn't have happened in our day."

This from a woman who had to leave her father at the age of four due to her mother's surrender to consumption. She was raised by a stentorian aunt and had adopted her black and white set of absolutes about morality and hadn't yet had them challenged by the actions of her own family. Her liberalization was still to come.

"They should do something about it," offered another without feeling any obligation to specify who 'they' were.

"No good will come of it, mark my words," from the pessimist whose own life underpinned her certainty that another disaster was waiting round the corner.

"Ah sure God is good."

This handing over of responsibility to a greater power ended the conversation and allowed them to move on to other snippets of gossip while they waited for more sherry to be slipped through by the seeming disembodied hand of the barman. No money changed hands. The drink would be added to the weekly book under another heading.

Gradually there were whisperings that Robert P was a homosexual. He kept himself to himself and showed no interest in the available spinsters in the village. He didn't go to Mass or hurling matches, both almost qualifying as mortal sins. He went on solitary walks up the mountain road as far as the fence stile locally known as the 'broken sit down'. Some of the local men sitting in the local round the spruce fire cradling the warmth from their hot whiskeys and watching the brown smoke from their Sweet Afton cigarettes curl up the soot laden chimney scornfully suggested that he wrote poetry.

"None of them sorts of fellas are right in the head," was the consensus view. He went for two pints each night and sat in the corner on his own responding if spoken to but initiating very little beyond observations on the weather. Of course the word homosexual wasn't used.

Billy gradually started visiting the house. It wasn't because Joey was a friend of his. Joey was about seven years older than him and he had grown up a bit wild. He missed school on a regular basis and was often in trouble for stealing things.

"Sure why wouldn't he and that fella looking after him, if that's what you could call it," was the commonest explanation offered each time the local guard brought him home by the ear. Robert P's place in the order of things had been firmly established ensuring no threat to the series of absolutes that maintained the conservative status quo.

But Joey was handy when he did hang round with Billy and his friends. He was big like his father and he could reach blackberries higher up than anyone. If the gang from Billy's street wanted to take over the handball alley at the top of the town or the football field at the other end having Joey around encouraged other incumbents to leave quickly. He was also brilliant to have as your 'horse" in the jousting competitions that involved a small lad like Billy sitting on the shoulders of a bigger and hopefully stronger boy armed with a stick sword. First one to fall or cry out was the loser. Billy never lost with Joey as his partner. There was a picture of them in action on the site of the old dog pound in the tin box at home where pictures that didn't make it onto the wall or into albums were kept.

All that was in the past now as Joey was eighteen and had taken up more adult pastimes like drinking which offered him more opportunities to be in trouble. The reason Billy started going to the house was that Robert P had inherited a barbers business and had started cutting men and boys hair to supplement what the State deemed him worthy of receiving. What in fact happened was that the previous barber's sight was failing and he offered his hand clippers, combs and scissors to his next door neighbour. After a few cursory lessons in the only style on demand, short back and sides, he set up business during the daylight hours on a bar stool set in the middle of the front room to maximize the available light. Billy went there with his father and brother every couple of months to wince and complain as the clippers pinched and pulled his straight brown hair into some sort of shape. His father's balding pate which rarely saw daylight from under his cap offered less of a challenge. Because of the rumours no boys were allowed to go there alone.

One day Billy was sat on the high stool halfway through the ordeal while his brother and father waited their turn. He had decided to go first because he had plans to go snaring rabbits that evening and wanted to be ready to sell them to the man who visited the village on the following day to purchase the kill. An imperious knock rattled the front door. Billy looked at his father who was looking at Robert P. He glanced at the clock set alone in the middle of the wooden mantelpiece. It offered no obvious explanation for the loud intrusion. Robert P rubbed his hands together anxiously and eased open the front door which led directly from the front room to the street.

Billy peeped round Robert P's small frame.

The Garda Sergeant and constable that made up the village force stood alongside three bulky men dressed in civilian clothes. Until that day Billy thought detectives existed only in America and in the comics he bought each Thursday at the paper shop in the Main Street.

"Where's Joey?" asked the Sergeant wandering into the back room.

"What's he done now?" The answer came with an exhalation of resignation born of many previous situations.

Billy's father widened his eyes, his head tilted in an obvious warning to be quiet.

"Never mind that, where is he?"

"I don't know. He hasn't come in from school yet." His normally quiet monotone rose to a more shrill level.

"What's he been up to that takes five of you to deal with?"

"You'll know soon enough and then you won't want to know," said one of the three detectives gruffly. He turned to the others.

"I'll wait here in case he comes home. You go and search for him." He pushed past the small man without further invitation.

Robert P returned to the room, his soft hands shaking.

"You'll have to go," he said needlessly. Billy's father had already started ushering the two boys to the door.

"But I've only half a haircut," protested Billy as he was dragged from the high stool. His father picked up the clippers.

"I'll finish him at home and bring them back later."

That was the day that Billy's father decided to go to the Co-op and buy himself a pair of clippers.

"It'll save us money in the long run," he explained to Billy's mother who questioned the ability of a forestry worker to pick up such skills.

That was the day that Joey killed a 13 year old farmer's daughter on her way home from the village school and transformed her instantly from a 'good girl' to an angel having robbed her of any chance to be anything in between.

That was the day the light dimmed in her father's eyes.

That was the day that Joey, in one merciless moment completed his transformation from a 'wild young fella' to a demon.

That was the last day Robert P cut hair in the village.

That was the day that the curtains were again drawn in the flaking house up the road.

That was the day that Billy rescued the picture of himself sitting on Joey's shoulders from the tin box in the dressing table drawer and hid it in his secret place under the mattress of his bed. He knew he had to do it before his mother got hold of it and tried to wipe all associations with the monster.

Billy would look at the black and white photo now and again. You could never tell from his smile that he was a murderer. He wondered if the smile is lost as well as the life taken. His own smile seemed out of place, somehow irreverent to the memory of the dead girl.

But he held onto it. He knew that the ripples of shock, horror and hate would fade to the calm waters of rationalization. He knew that explanation would eventually shine through the clear lenses of hindsight. It had to if the closed society was to absorb and move on from this knife thrust to its self assurance and continuity.

He also knew that when that day came the photo would offer him a currency in the competitive years of growing up. The evidence was there in black and white. He had sat on a murderer's shoulders and smiled.

Anastasia

The commotion shifted Anastasia's gaze to the door of the house on the other side of the narrow cobbled street. What was Demetrious, the fat Greek doing? Two soldiers stood smoking, like a father and son, mildly interested. Demetrious was busily twisting a net cloth round a pomegranate while babbling in a mixture of Greek and German about the custom in Corfu of smashing this fruit on the doorstep.

"The amount of fruit that goes inside the threshold will show you the amount of good luck the house can expect in the coming year."

The soldiers laughed, taking long pulls from their cigarettes as he swung the net onto the red step. The cloth ripped with a squelch dumping most of the wine apple's fruit onto their shiny black boots. Anastasia jammed her hand in her mouth to plug the laugh swelling up inside her. For a moment nothing moved except the cigarette smoke rising lazily to the darkening sky. The older one reached towards a holster in his over tight belt. Demetrious beat him to the draw, whipping a white handkerchief from his waistcoat. He folded to his knees mopping up the fruit and wiping sweat from his red face onto his shirtsleeve.

"I am so sorry. Forgive me. Forgive me. Here, let me clean up the mess. Stupid bloody custom."

The soldier replaced his gun as Demetrious rose slowly and with his head bobbing up and down eased opened the dark wooden door. With a warning finger and a slap round the head they stepped inside. Demetrious mopped his forehead with the stained cloth, leaning for support against the closed half of the door, dragging in air in great gasps. He glanced in Anastasia's general direction. She pressed herself back into the shadows. When she looked again the fat man was gone and the door to her old home was once again closed. She crept forward and picked small lumps of fruit from the footpath. The sweet juice made her smile. She pushed the door open enough to see past the threshold. There was no fruit inside. She smiled again. No luck in that house next year.

Anastasia liked to sneak back in the twilight hours to see their old house. She carefully wrapped herself round the corner, peering up through the gloom, remembering the first floor apartment where her parents and older brother and sister had lived. The whole street sat in the shade of the new fortress in the old town of Corfu. They had been driven out by the German and Italian invaders. Anastasia hadn't heard her mother's screams or the two shots that killed her father. She had returned home to find her mother sprawled silently on the dusty footpath with her brother and sister enveloped in her black apron. Anastasia didn't know why he had died. No one answered her questions. After her brother ran away to the mountains of the north she stopped asking.

On these night time visits she noticed differences. There were no families going in and out. The heavy panelled door to the shadowy hallway with its broad marble staircase now opened for older girls with garish clothes and swaying bodies. They tottered on the cobbles in their high heels, arms linked, laughing as their scarlet finger nails flicked tobacco specks from their full lips. Anastasia knew that men liked them. As the girls strutted down the streets they were followed by catcalls and whistles. When she had tried walking like that people only laughed. With a whip of their hips and a glance tossed over their shoulders they ignored the few young men who had not fled to the mountains. For soldiers they stopped and posed, allowing themselves to be touched. As they walked away they swore in their own tongue while still smiling and waving. Anastasia looked on, confused. Old women crossed themselves inside their black shawls. Old men just gazed at the ground.

Orange shafts from the setting sun wrapped the horizon in a gold ribbon. Anastasia turned away. The high steepled church clanged its nightly warning one hour before the curfew. She had to get back to her uncle's house before he missed her and before her mother and her sister Martha returned home from their nightly hunt for food. He lived alone on the first floor above his spice and fish shop. Anastasia's mother had said he was too mean to marry. He had boasted to his drinking friends through his brown stained teeth when he had taken them off the streets a year before. What he didn't tell them was that the three of them had to make do with the small room under the eaves at the top of the house. A single round window high on the gable end looked over the brown tiled roofs of the sprawl of twisting streets. He neglected to mention that his sister in law had to keep the whole house instead of paying rent.

The smell of fish was everywhere. It seeped into the yellowing plaster on the walls. It rode on the breeze in the passageways and stairways. It caked her uncle's clothes and oiled his streaky grey hair. Anastasia didn't like him at first, now she hated him. She imagined him as Spiro the shark. She trembled when he barged into their room often at rising and resting times, leering at her mother and sister as they covered themselves with the nearest item of clothing. He had taken the key from the door lock. He found ways of rubbing himself against her mother, his greasy hands moving over her spare frame, her mother feigning a smile while cautiously peeling his hands away. Sometimes, after he left, her mother had vomited in the bucket that served as their night time toilet.

They were barred from his shop. Anastasia got used to his comings and goings and had started sneaking in when he went to the tavern round the corner during the afternoon closure. She loved to walk along the sloped counter and look at the spices piled to peaks in the locally made straw baskets. Red chillies gave a clear warning of the fire inside, golden sweet cumin sat alongside warm cream ginger, straw coloured coriander seeds near the green cardamom. She liked to mix up the light brown cinnamon sticks with strands of orange saffron. She would wander from the hot display to the other end of the right angled counter where fish of all sizes lay on granite slabs bedded in ice chipped from the blocks delivered each morning. The dead eyes of sardines, mackerel and anchovies seemed to follow her as she walked. She imagined lobsters clamping their sharp pincers on her uncle's fingers. Occasionally a large swordfish lay at the back, mouth open, as if ready to devour the frozen shoals of squid and shrimp lying in front. She had stolen a couple of bags of red pepper and some white paper bags that were used to wrap small amounts of spices. She hid them under the thin mattress that bore the marks of the rusting springs of her metal bed. During the day she went to demolished buildings and carefully scraped red brick dust into a discarded tea tin. If anyone looked she pretended she was writing in the dust. When she thought her mother and sister were asleep she sat cross legged in the quartered moonlight on the deep window recess and carefully mixed the dust with enough pepper to convince enquiring noses. She twisted each bag carefully to protect the precious contents. On market days she arranged her hoard on a shallow wooden tray held by string which at the day's end left its red imprint on her thin neck. She used her wide brown eyes and winsome smile to persuade shoppers. They rarely checked the bags. She moved from place to place developing her ability to remember faces. One day a large German lady peered back with a look of half recognition. She looked away. When she looked again Anastasia was safe in the shade of a convenient doorway.

One afternoon, at the usual time, Anastasia picked her way through the cluttered shop. She reached into an open barrel of sardines, stuffing her mouth with the oily salted fish. Any chance to eat had to be taken, mealtimes often passed without food. The hunger pangs were always there, grasping her stomach. Her mother had made three new holes in the belt of her dress since coming to live with her uncle. Sometimes when no food was found her mother would stay out all night. In the morning she would have small amounts of money. She never said where the money came from. Her head down silence was matched by the girls knowing not to ask where she had been. She always spent longer on her knees by her bed the following evening asking God's forgiveness.

Spiro leaped from behind the high brown counter. He grabbed her hair and slapped her hard across the face. Her nose dripped red and her eyes filled. The stinging tears did not overflow. Crying was weakness. She had learnt not to show it. The half chewed fish shot out of her pulsing mouth. He trod the mess with his dirty brown boots into the gaps between the chipped floor tiles.

"Hungry are you? Hungry enough to steal from your uncle? Enough to eat this?"

His shouting filled her head as he forced her down to the mess on the floor

"Eat," he screamed "Eat, or by God and his Holy mother you and your ungrateful family will be back on the streets tonight."

She scraped the filthy mess up and pushed it into her mouth. She closed her eyes and lips tight and forced herself to swallow. Her stomach heaved and pushed it back up to fill the space behind her clenched teeth. The sour smell filled her nostrils. Three times she swallowed before she could relax and breathe.

"I'll give you something to remember this by." He jerked her to her feet, reached behind the wooden counter and grabbed a large pair of black scissors. The pain in her eyes pulsed as his grip tightened. She heard the snip of the scissors, the pressure on her scalp relaxed and was replaced by a pain on top of her ear where he had nipped her. He held her hair like a trophy.

"That will teach you. Explain that to your mother. Tell her how you dishonour your uncle, how you throw his kindness in his face." He pushed her out of the shop into the damp passageway and threw her hair after her. Anastasia got on her knees and gathered her strewn tresses, seeking out single hairs, unsure of why she was doing it, afraid to leave any behind.

Her mother held her and shook her head as the story catapulted from her daughter's mouth, her breath exuding the aftertaste of sardines and gastric juices. Anastasia waited for her mother to go and challenge her uncle. Instead her mother said

"We will have to do something with your hair. You can't go round looking like that."

Anastasia stayed silent, no longer sure who had been at fault. Her mother gently cut the other side a little bit longer.

"It will soon grow back and no one will notice," her mother assured her.

Anastasia dropped the hair she had collected, rubbing her hands together to get rid of the single threads stuck to her oily hands. She vowed never to have long hair again. It had been used to hurt her, to force her to eat like the scrawny dogs that roamed the streets. She stood in front of the biggest piece of the cracked mirror on the back of their bedroom door and practiced head leaning until she was satisfied that her hair looked even on both sides. Now nine months later she could hold her head straight.

She heard a girl's scream before she turned the corner. Two young men clattered past her.

"Germans! Run."

She wheeled round and scurried down a narrow alley. The noise faded quickly and she slowed to catch her breath. The old buildings with their cupped lattice shutters seemed to murmur to each other, pointing her out. A smell of warm baking drifted in the space. She inched along the wall, her bony fingers marking the way. The smell got stronger. A half open door at the back of a warmly painted building beckoned her. Her caution was swept away by the nearness of relief from the gnawing pain in her stomach. With no more than a cursory glance she pushed open the door and stepped over the wooden lintel. The courtyard was strewn with abandoned furniture. A gunshot from the distance cracked the air and made her jump. The smell was coming from an open door at the other side of the quadrangle. As she reached it she heard voices, German voices. She looked round, eyes wide, looking for a hiding place. The door swinging in the evening breeze on the other side of the square was now too far away. She jumped into a large brown wardrobe. It smelled of emptiness, like her grandfather's room just before he had died. She drew her finger to her lips as she pulled the door inward and shut out the early evening light.   The latch clicked noisily. She stretched her lean arms. Her fingers barely touched the sides. A pinprick of light squeezed in past the metal key welded in the lock. Anastasia focused on the dust particles spinning in the light beam. She was used to darkness that held on to the warmth of the sun. Each evening as the light faded the shutters of the high buildings were flung open. The streets echoed with the hustle and bustle of small shops and street stalls reopening. Children squealed as they ran in and out of dark doorways; chasing feral cats that scurried under food stalls trying to filch fallen scraps. The fading of the day was now a cold perilous time ruled by the occupiers. The talking hands weaving words in the street lights to the lilting tune of her people's voices had been silenced. The staccato tone and strange words of the foreigner now kept tune with their stamping, polished jackboots on the shiny, uneven cobbles. She clutched her stomach trying to stop the rumble bursting out. She had eaten nothing since the lump of bread and anchovies she had stolen the day before last. She silently spoke her mother's words.

"Hold your head up, girl. Don't show them you are hungry. Your stomach doesn't have windows."

Her straining ears and eyes sensed no relief from the pervasive blackness. It seemed to be taking her from the light to itself, devouring her silently. The tears spilled from her creased eyes. Her arms shook, seeming to rattle without sound in the dress she had worn for weeks, its flowers faded to grey, the collar lined with dried sweat. She had to have more light, to force the gloom back from her shoulders, back into the corners where it could do her no harm. Her held breath pushed on the belt that grabbed the folds of the oversized dress. She peeled her sweating hands apart and pushed on the door with one hesitant finger. The shaft of light widened, warming her hand and one side of her peeping face. No sound except her heart. She pushed again and stepped on tip toe out onto the grey stone tiles of the courtyard. She glanced upward to the darkening sky. *It must still be before curfew,* she thought.

She crossed to the half open door. Her stomach screamed her hunger. The odour got stronger. Her vigilance was brushed aside by the nearness of relief from the gnawing pain. She dashed to the pile of fresh buns on a baking tray set on a wooden table that seemed to fill the kitchen. She took a mouth cramming bite from one in her left hand while her right packed the two front pockets in her dress. She went to take a second, urgent bite. Her head was yanked backwards. Her teeth crashed together, her eyes watered and the force of the pull on her hair knocked her to the stone floor. She watched helplessly as the buns flew from her pockets and rolled out of reach of her flailing hands.

The German boy was big and fat, shouting words she could not understand. He twisted the neck of her dress round one podgy hand and heaved her stumbling and screaming back out through the door. Her knees grazed and bled on the rough ground as each wrench sent her flying. He flung her against the grey swill bins that held the waste from the nearby houses. With his free hand he pulled the cover off the nearest grey bin. The metal clang on stone reverberated round the enclosure, echoing, deafening, but bringing no one who might help her. The world was deaf. The stench of rotten food was overpowering. He moved his hand back and forth to his mouth in a cupping motion while pretending to chew. Anastasia's eyes widened in terror as she realized what was about to happen. Her mouth was open, screaming for her mother as he pushed her face into the stinking semi solid mulch. It was dark again. All sound stopped. Her mouth nose and ears filled. She struggled in vain. Then her head was jerked back into the light. She snorted air through her partly blocked nose. Her stomach heaved and with a rib jarring contraction she vomited all over his clothes. The pressure on her scalp relaxed as he stood, hands flailing, searching for some way to deal with the cloying mess that dripped to his feet. Anastasia seized her chance and raced through the door in the wall to the narrow safety of the adjoining streets. She heard the door bang only once behind her.

She had reached the far end of the street from her uncle's house when the nearby church bells clanged their last warning. 9 o clock. The curfew hour. Doors banged as the town battened down another night of occupation. As Anastasia sidled along, her fingers spidering along the walls, a wink in the gutter caught her eye. She tiptoed away from the wall. The shiny handgun was jammed, barrel down, in the metal grate of a storm drain. During heavy rain showers she used to make boats of twigs wrapped with different coloured scraps of cloth with her friends and race them on the rivulets gushing alongside the footpaths. The last boat in each race was allowed to drop into the depths below the drain. The races continued until there was only one boat left. The gun looked like the ones she had seen in the soldiers' holsters. Her right hand closed round the cold metal butt. She placed it carefully in the pocket of her dress. The street remained empty. The weight bounced against her leg as she eased through the wooden back door of her uncle's house and ran down the dank passageway to the back stairs that led to their room. She barged through the bedroom door into the murky light from the oil lamp on the dressing table. She stiffened as her eyes swept the scene in front of her. Martha lay curled up on her bed, knees pulled up under her chin, sobbing, her body shaking, bedclothes strewn on the floor. She was naked. Her uncle stood red faced and barefoot near the bed, the black tangle of hair on his chest uncovered, his fat belly overhanging his trousers, his braces dangling at either side near his knees. Her mother stood beside him, back to Anastasia, screaming from inside her loose coat and faded scarf.

"What have you done? You filthy pig, she is only a girl, your brother's girl. You bastard, Get out, Get out."

Her mother swung round as Anastasia slammed the door. Tears etched shiny tracks over her dark skin; drawn tight over her bony face. Despair and fear framed her red rimmed green eyes.

"Oh my God, what happened to you? Where have you been? I was out looking for you. I left your sister alone."

The gunshot filled the space, drowning out all other sounds. Anastasia almost lost her balance from the kickback. Her arm jerked upward, loosening her grip on the gun. Martha screeched and sat bolt upright on the bed, her palms pressed to her ears, eyes shut tight. Her uncle's hands moved to his chest. He looked astounded as he folded to the floor face down. A crimson pool spread outward filling the dusty gaps between the floorboards. His arms and legs twitched like dying fish and then he was still. Anastasia turned to face her mother, now rooted to the spot, her mouth and eyes wide open.

Close the shutters, she thought. *Your stomach may have no windows but your eyes do.*

"I found some bread. I was trying to get home."

She unclenched her left hand. The bun, with one bite gone, lay flattened and moist on her palm. She broke the bread and offered a piece to her mother and sister.

Green Cups and Saucers

He swerved outward to avoid the street sweeper's cart that had been abandoned at the road edge and had suddenly appeared as a yellow blur between the swish swish of the windscreen wipers.

"What the bloody hell," he shouted to the empty leather look seats in his new lease car. A smaller car on the other side of the road moved to seek safety on the opposite footpath. Another flash of colour picked out the man sat in the bus shelter. He pulled the car into the side, scrabbled round the unfamiliar dashboard and put on the flashers. Striding imperiously back down the footpath he rehearsed the piece of his mind he was about to deliver.

"Nice and dry in here are you? Typical council worker! Looking after number one. If you had a second brain cell you'd be dangerous."

His head dipped against the driving rain as he neared the shelter which promised two numbered buses to Maidstone, the County town of Kent. He flicked water from his neat brown hair and beard already regretting the fact that his raincoat lay dry on the back seat. The man sitting alone on the green metal seat looked familiar. He was tall, angular, head face down, his hair a few weeks late for the barbers. Balanced on his thin knees was an open tin of Golden Virginia tobacco. His calloused hands extending from the oversize reflective yellow council coat were clumsily rolling a cigarette. It was then that Billy noticed the red Rizla cigarette papers. That was what triggered the memory, the identification, and the person.

"'Cedric is it you?" Billy asked with more than enough assurance.

The man lifted his head reluctantly. Stray wisps of blond and grey tinged hair draped over the large glasses that hung askew on his long red nose. His eyes narrowed behind the dirty lenses, concentrating, suspicious, his hands struggling to keep control of the open tobacco tin and papers.

"Mr. Griffin. Billy. Long time no see."   The smile of recognition broke over his wrinkled spare face as he moved over. Billy accepted the silent invitation and sat down on the narrow green tin seat. The cold pierced his lightweight suit trousers.

Cedric was an only child. He had been slow from birth, late walking talking and learning. He had never known his father and his mother had never felt inclined or obliged to tell him about 'that waster'.

"The less you know about him the better. All you need to know is that he left us high and dry in this mess."

They lived in a small red brick council house in a small estate set under the exhalations from the tall grey chimneys of the local paper mills. She tried to nag Cedric to some sort of achievement all the way through school. He wasn't up to it and had to leave early. One Sunday he reacted to yet another upbraiding about his general uselessness and threw his dinner through the small kitchen window into their tiny back yard. His mother was appalled, next doors dog was delighted. He ate the dinner, she called the police. They took one look at him and took him to the local mental hospital in the unfortunately named Barming area of Maidstone. After three days of observation on their part and total fear and non-cooperation on his part he was diagnosed as being 'mentally defective' and admitted to a large institution, Leybourne Grange, ten miles away for his own and society's protection, one of eleven hundred others drawn from the South East of England and South London Boroughs. His mother adjusted their relationship to Sunday afternoon visiting hours within the grounds as the Medical Superintendent was unwilling to sign the slip that would allow him to step through the large metal gates that served as entrance and exit.

That's where they had met. To be precise Billy first met him when a large cumbersome soccer full back had decided to negate his slight frame speed advantage by taking the legs from under him. Cedric brought the all-important bottle of water to help get him back to scoring ways. Billy was playing on the hospital soccer team for two reasons. He liked sport but of equal importance if you were representing the hospital you were considered to be on duty. As he was good at sport most of his three years nurse training consisted of a four day week. Maggie Thatcher was too busy sorting out the miners to notice what was going on in the rest of the public sector. Their paths overlapped a lot after that as they both exercised work and social roles in the self-contained community that was the hospital. Cedric was one of a small number of 'high grade' patients who had achieved a modicum of status, an impersonation of normality, that while still far short of regular society was far in advance of what the other one thousand plus patients had to endure. He had his own room attached to a ward housing forty clients. He had his own small cooker and kettle. This was unheard of for the patients. Kitchens were one of four rooms in each ward that were always locked; the others being the office, the staff room and the laundry cupboard. Kitchens were out of bounds in case of accidents. You drank when it was prepared, not when you felt like it. Cedric had a job as a porter. The only difference was that he didn't get paid the full amount for it.

"It would interfere with his benefits," insisted the Finance Officer who also ran the Social Club with his wife and who years later would be convicted of siphoning off patients benefits into his own account. His wife didn't know and left him. The most prized possession for Cedric was a little laminated card that said he was a member of the Staff Sports and Social Club. He had his fees waived while the rest had them deducted from their wages. Cedric was known by everyone and like the rest of the Social Club members, after a few pints, would go back to his institution, the ward annex while they went to theirs, the three story five hundred roomed nurses home. His shuffling stride from his knock knees carried him back and forth with ease between the otherwise strictly guarded borders between staff and patients. His amiable nature guaranteed a degree of respect. Occasionally a wind up merchant would show why all those years before Cedric's dinner had gone through the window. Then Cedric would not be seen for a couple of days.

"Long time no see is right. It must be seven years. How are you?" He pulled his coat round him as a gust of wind shook the Perspex shelter. The original reason for stopping floated back gently.

"Look Cedric. It might be an idea to pull your cart up onto the path. It might cause an accident."

Cedric shuffled to his feet, placed the unlit cigarette on the seat and went out to do as he was asked. The well engrained habit of obeying commands was still well and truly thriving.

Billy placed his hand over the cigarette to prevent it blowing away.

"Still using red Rizlas I see."

"They are the only ones that will give you a proper smoke," came the reply Billy had last heard seven years previously as he prepared to leave the hospital after qualifying. Cedric's contention that the colour of the packet influenced the outcome was one of his defining characteristics that anyone who knew him well recognized.

"Where did you go when you left," he enquired while looking away in the time honoured fashion of people in the subservient position. The hospital gates might be closed. The weeds might be gaining dominance on the previously meticulously kept flower beds. The paint might be peeling round the rusty chains and padlocks of the ward doors. But their mutual roles were still in place. They both understood them. They could communicate via them. The wind and rain swept bus shelter was not the place to start dismantling them.

Cedric picked up the cigarette and offered him the tin.

"I gave up a couple of years ago." The tin scraped back along the metal seat.

"There was a time when you would have one," he ventured

"Different days," Billy answered." I went on to do General training and then moved to Yorkshire. And now I'm back and live in Gillingham."

"Did you marry that nurse you were going out with?"

"Which one," Billy smiled. There was no reaction from the other end of the seat.

"The blond girl. Nice girl. Always said hello"'

"I did," he confirmed

"What's your job now?"

"I've come back to close down the rest of the Grange, at least to take the Maidstone people out. The place is half empty as it is. I see you got out early."

Cedrics demeanour changed as if the wind had suddenly swung round to the North.

"I had no bloody choice but to leave. I was never asked what I wanted. They came for the high grades first because they thought we could handle it. Do you know how I found out that I might be going?"

Billy was surprised. This chance meeting because of a badly parked cart, this casual conversation about filling in the intervening years had veered off the road into a lane that challenged everything he was about at that time. He had jumped at the chance of leading a project to get patients from his old training hospital into community settings. He couldn't wait to leave the place after qualifying and couldn't wait to get back and close it. It had never dawned on him that it might not be right for everyone.

The idea of looking at the watch and racing off to a concocted meeting suddenly reared its ugly head. Something not in Cedric's eyes stopped him. They were empty.

"How did you find out?"

"Remember the villa I lived next to. Well one morning I was told I would have to start taking my meals back in the dining room with the others. Remember before I could take them to my room. I sat at the table and when the student came round with the dinners I asked him what was going on."

"You're one of the green cups and saucers. We have to watch to see you have good living skills before you go out into the community."

"That was the first he had heard about the hospital closing."

"So what happened then?"

"After a few months I was told they had a flat for me here, and a job. I packed my bags without even seeing the place. The reason they brought me here was that I used to live here. They never asked me if I wanted to come back."

"Isn't it nice to live here among people you know?' Billy offered already fearing the answer".

Cedric paused and gave him a look of disbelief.

"The few people who remember me only remember one thing about me, the reason I was taken away from home in the first place. They think I might hurt them. They never say anything. But you can see it in the way they look at the ground when I am passing, that's if they haven't already crossed the road before I get near them. The rest of the place just ignores me. I live in a small flat, on my own. It's a council flat. I'm on the fifth floor. I don't like living up in the air. I have no garden just a small ledge with a couple of window boxes. It's not the same having nowhere to sit out. I sometimes go to the park but I get funny looks and have to leave. The people upstairs are always changing. Some of them are real rowdy, especially the kids. They blackguard me sometimes and if I say anything they say they will tell their parents that I touched them. You know I never do that sort of thing don't you Billy? But who is going to believe me."

The silence caught Billy unaware. He nodded encouragingly to Cedric.

"You used to like a pint. Do you still have one? Cider was your tipple if I remember?"

"The Social Club in the Grange closed two years ago. I used to go back there for a pint. I knew the people there. If I go for a pint now nobody talks to me. I have to sit in a corner on my own. I prefer to bring a few cans from the takeaway and sit indoors with a video."

Billy changed tack with the practised ease of his profession. The windy shelter was fast becoming a therapy room.

"What about the job. Isn't it good to be earning a bit of money?"

"I don't like it. Up and down them streets. Every day the same bloody thing. You wouldn't want to see the things I have to pick up. These gloves don't protect your stomach from churning. The kids know I was in the Grange. They stole my brush a couple of times. The Council took the cost of the new one out of my pay."

He re lit the cigarette stub drawing deeply on the relief. Billy sat, silent, unable to fill the space, unable to offer comfort, any skills he had redundant in the face of this sad reality.

"Once I chased them, the little buggers, shouted at them, tried to make them go away. The next day a cop car pulled up in the street and warned me I would end up in Oakwood if I carried on. Everyone was watching. They were nodding their heads. I was crying. I didn't want to meet people after that because I know what they will say."

"So what do you do? Who do you meet." Billy was stepping deeper and deeper into a morass that he knew he could not navigate safely.

"I worked it out, the bus tables. I know when they are due. So I make sure I am near them when nobody will be waiting."

"So you're not here just sheltering from the rain."

"No," he laughed as if Billy had missed the obvious."This is where I have my afternoon tea break. I can have fifteen minutes but I sometimes have more. I have my morning break in Swan Street and my lunch in the High Street. All the girls from the offices are out having their lunch at that time. I like to watch them. They remind me of the nurses in the hospital. I have to make sure they don't notice me. That way I keep out of trouble."

Billy put his head in his hands glancing at his watch, casting round for a gentle exit.

"The worst thing that ever happened was closing the Grange. All my friends are gone back to where they came from. They never even gave us their addresses. If they had done that I could have asked someone to write a letter for me. If I got one back I could have asked someone to read it out to me. Do you remember? You and the lads on the team used to do it for me. That's gone now. I bump into some of the staff who live round here now and again. They're always in a hurry. It's not the same."

Billy sat in abject silence at Cedric's evaluation of the holy cow of Community Care, his holy cow, his reason for getting up on a Monday morning.

Cedric placed the tobacco tin in the large pocket of his coat and dragged on the large gloves thrown under the seat.

"Time's up. I have to go. Nice to see you Billy." With that he was gone, trundling the squeaky cart down the street into his predictable sad future.

Billy sat, stunned, his whole belief system so carefully assembled in theory and experience strewn before him like the spilled contents of Cedric's tobacco tin. How could something designed to wash away the monster of institutional care leave someone in this state, alone, ridiculed, afraid, and without status.

They had dismissed his community because it didn't tie in with their view of the world. They forgot it was all he had. They had pulled it apart, dispersed it and replaced it with nothing. How many more Cedric's had been given a green cup and saucer and been told "Come on it's time to go."

An older woman, well wrapped in her mackintosh and see through plastic hat and wrestling with a floral umbrella, entered the shelter. She placed her basket carefully by her side while assessing the man next to her in the smart suit with the coat collar turned up.

Billy stood up, consulted the timetable, smiled, and headed back to the flashing lights and safety of his car and future.

Changing Forever

The door to the shared passage leading from the street to the back gardens slammed annoyingly and without rhythm in the wind gusting from the moors at the top of the steep street. Each squall threw stray drops of rain into the passage to continue rusting the old bike thrown against the wall. The nine o clock newsreader competed with the whining wind in the small front room of the stone built terraced house. Clouds raced past in the darkening sky outside the net curtains. Old locals at their crown green bowling had it that even on a fine day clouds were always black by the time they left Yorkshire; suffused with the exhalations of the pit chimneys. Exhortations from the woman of the house filtered through the thick stone built walls encouraging their two boys to complete their homework. Their protests were met with a re-emergence of her native Geordie accent. This was enough to silence further argument.

"If that bloody woman in London has her way the only geography they will need to know is how to get to the nearest unemployment office. It won't be hard, just look for the longest queue." I was confused momentarily until I realized his comment was directed at the television. The two year old family photograph sat on top still waiting for a decision as to the best place to hang it.

Underneath the grocers daughter's face in her clipped Home Counties accent reiterated her determination to rid the country of unions who believed that withdrawal of labour and holding the country to ransom was the only effective negotiation tool. She didn't mention the coal miners by name, she didn't have to. It was now three weeks into the miners' strike and the list of pits on strike had not yet reached the maximum.

"What the fuck does she understand about us up here in the North? Bloody Southerners." He looked slightly apologetically at me remembering I had brought my southern wife into the wilderness above the Watford Gap; the unmarked dividing line between bowler hats and cloth caps.

"Can't she see she is going to destroy not just jobs, but communities? She doesn't give a toss about any of us."

His frustration settled in black ever present shadows that framed his large brown eyes. He crumpled the newspaper effortlessly in his big black lined hands and hurled it in the general direction of a bin in the far corner of the room. It dropped under the curtains with the rest of the overflow.

"I'm fed up of reading this shite. He says this; she says that, Thatcher telling us to do one thing, Scargill telling us to do the opposite. Both of them threatening us with the consequences of following the other. How are you supposed to make any sense of it? And in the meantime we're sitting here living on strike pay and handouts."

This by the standards of this man of few words was a veritable speech. He sighed out the emotion that fuelled the outburst. His large frame shrunk into the floral patterned armchair.

He had, according to his biased mother, been good in school. She never tired of telling willing and unwilling audiences that Maths was his forte. Unlike his easy going father she harboured all sorts of ambitions for him. Unfortunately for her his only ambition was to earn good money from the time he left school. This would help to pay for the things important to an eighteen year old brought up on a diet of his inferior place in the North South economic divide of England. At six feet five and not shy of work he was perfect for the pits of his West Yorkshire home. The money was good. He promised himself ten years to save enough money to finance the master plan; his own house, his own building business. He got locked into the normal life rhythms and the master plan was left undelivered. Like others he never challenged the presumption that because people would always need energy they would always need coal. The emergence of the nuclear fuel option, although noted, never registered as a real threat because of a naïve belief that the dependence of local communities on the industry would never be sacrificed, would always be a good enough reason for it to carry on. He forgot that not everyone had socialist convictions. A job for life. The pit head at the top of the grey stone and red brick mining villages would always be more important than the church, the shift hooter always louder than the evensong bell, the pit brass band always sweeter than the choir.

Underpinning all of this was his surrender of individual responsibility for his future to the collective bargaining methodology of an increasingly radical union that promised continuity.

"I can't see anything clearly anymore. I'm like a sheep standing too close to the thorn bush. You're well out of this mess. What do you think?"

His brown eyes peered at me from under his heavy eyebrows, his head still half inclined to the floor. He always looked as if he was peering over invisible glasses. His invitation was at once complimentary in terms of asking my opinion but also challenging given my natural propensity to play the part of devil's advocate.

We had met through one of those amazing coincidences that would almost help you to believe in an all-powerful being. I had moved with my wife from Kent on completion of nurse training in order to buy a house. We couldn't afford the mortgage on one in the more affluent southeast. We hadn't been in West Yorkshirelong enough to make any friends. As a treat for all our efforts we had decided to go camping in the beautiful mountain and lake country of Northumberland.

With the optimism of youth we had ignored all ranges of weather forecasts. Two days later we were walking the mile from the campsite to the bus stop, the rain obliterating the mountains and replenishing the natural reservoirs at a healthy rate and me vowing I would never be caught under canvas again. A car splashed by.

"That looks like our neighbours car," said my much more observant wife. With that the car slowed and a lifelong friendship began. We went 150 miles to meet people who were four doors lower down the steep street on which we lived. Although we both understood the rules of our friendship I had noticed the deterioration in his normally sanguine approach to life's troubles since the start of the strike. Walking on eggshells was never a skill I had practiced, never mind master. His wife peered round the panelled door, took one silent, understanding look at us and left without her usual good humoured comment.

"The men want to be left alone for now." She offered no further explanation as she ushered the complaining boys back into the room with the small black and white telly.

I was a community nurse for people with a mental handicap, now promoted, in language at least, to intellectual disability. This allowed me to take a totally different standpoint. I could look on at what was happening with a certain complacent concern. I covered many of the outlying villages and towns which had varying dependencies on the industry in question. I had taken to delivering food parcels collected and rationed by the tireless miners' wives, mothers, co-habitees and fiancées. While their men stood round on stamping cold picket lines and in interminable union meetings considering what should be done their women got on with what needed doing. Each morning, on the way to work I would pick up my list of drop offs with instructions to either knock and wait or just drop at the front door and ring the bell depending on the perceived pride of the families involved. This helped augment ever shrinking resources and salved the slight guilt of those of us who remained relatively unscathed by the widening conflict. Our little bit for this particular war effort. With a suitably clear conscience I decided to go for broke.

"Take this any way you want. Your problem isn't just Thatcher, it's Scargill as well."

"What are you talking about? He was the one who warned us about what she was up to. Without him where would we be?"

"She's the immutable force and he's the immovable object. She's got business, power and a big majority in the House of Commons on her side and what does he do. He refuses to negotiate. He won't be moved and she's not for turning. And in the meantime day by day it's getting harder for you to look after your family. It might be alright on the picket line with your mates supping the subsidised lager from the publicans terrified of losing your trade but what is it like when you come home."

His wife and mine, good friends, had talked about the situation. She had filled me in on their situation.

"They're three months behind on the mortgage. His mother has lent her some money to pay the arrears. She daren't tell him. If this goes on much longer they're going to be in dire straits. And you know what he's like. Stubborn as a mule. Thinks he will be a scab if he walks away or goes to the pits where the other union has continued to work." I continued my analysis of his situation.

"The only thing wrong with Thatcher is the way she is going about this. She can only be ruthless because she has no credible opposition. And who finished her so called socialist opposition. The Unions. Remember the winter of discontent. Remember the power cuts, water shortages, no newspapers, no bloody ambulances. A socialist government trying to placate its socialist supporters. Even with a good majority they hadn't the balls to tell you to go and jump in the lake with your outlandish wage claims. You'd swear you were the only ones worth paying. The rest of us never got a look in. You screwed the country and when the country got the chance in the election it screwed you. How many union members voted against Labour? And now what have you got. A grocer's daughter with a plum in her mouth who thinks the only effort is that of the individual and thinks of you lot as a mob holding the rest of us to ransom."

"You sound like a Thatcher fan."

"Is that all you can do; insult me? I can't stand her. But people like her have to get their power from somewhere and I think you will be better able to suss all this mess out if you realize that you and your union buddies have made a contribution to it. You thought all you had to do was pay your dues and you were safe. Isn't that also an abuse of power when you don't consider the consequence of your actions on others?

"You might be right to some degree, but it still doesn't make it right."

"What's right got to do with it? Will it be any consolation to you that you were right when the Halifax come to repossess your house and sell it on for less than what you owe them on the mortgage? Arthur bloody Scargill won't turn up at your door to pay your debts. You lot think you are fighting for the whole country. Martyrs are usually named. There's only room for a few."

"I was thinking about going out on my own in the building trade. You know, set up a company. One of the lads at work is interested in coming in with me."

"Maggie would be proud of you." I ducked as his slipper flew at me.

"Look," I said trying to ease the situation "The weakness with collectives like unions is that they are made up of individuals.

Now some of them might be Sun readers and worse still believe what they read. They're the sort that will keep Scargill in power and ultimately help Maggie to win. They have no plan B and they don't demand that their leaders come up with one. What have you been offered if you lose? Feck all." The expression from my Irish childhood escaped causing him to smile. "Does it say in your union book that you have to give up the capacity to think independently to become a member? Are you not allowed to make your own decisions anymore? Remember there's more than you to think about. You only have one life. Do you want to spend the next ten years reminiscing about the great struggle over the couple of pints a week you can afford?"

He shook his head in resignation.

"I should have known better than to ask you. Do you ever just go along with what someone else says?"

"Only her indoors."

He never really asked my opinion again. I would have loved to think that I could have changed his mind. His wife found a simpler method. After pleading with him time and time again she packed her and the kids' bags and placed them without comment inside the front door under the stairs.

 "Work it out for yourself." was the only explanation offered to his demand. This confused him. He was used to other women who were sticking with their men in the face of ever mounting present debts and bleaker futures. She was never one to be part of the pack, never shy about making a decision. Now the consequences of his actions were all wrapped up in four canvas bags inside the hall door. His sons' excitement at going on a holiday to their Nan and Grandad's seemed to mock his own despair at the worsening situation.

Maggie's and Arthur's continuing widening of their ideological gap became less and less applicable in his own house. The battle, like all battles, became more about personal survival than a valued contribution to the cause. He became less available for the picket line. Nine o clock at night became the time when the telly was switched off and the front room empty. In the end he stepped outside the pack and decided.

"Fuck em. If I'm going to survive I'll have to do it on my own." The bags were unpacked and their lives rearranged into their familiar places.

Thatcher closed the coal industry, the price she was willing to pay to crush the unions. Communities were changed irrevocably. Scargill's high pitched voice faded to anonymity. There was no way back from that defeat.

My friend, like others, survived. They changed. They became reliant on their own efforts to make their way in life. Their confidence in community and collective expression was consigned to the parameters of rugby league and cricket grounds. Traditional allegiance to place, people and class were discarded. In its place came floating alliances forged from concepts of the greatest benefit to themselves. Mutual benefit was expressed through their Building Society accounts. They repeated the Faustian trade over and over in this life, unwilling to wait or settle for the promised eternal reward. Putting up with their lot collectively, the cement that bound their communities, crumbled in the drying air of self obsession. Without realizing it they became more right wing than people who had never espoused socialist beliefs.

Tolerance of difference was regarded as weakness, weakness in others as draining of their efforts.

Our arguments changed, our friendship changed, everything changed.

Cornelius

He loomed out of the half-light of dusk as I pulled the car onto the pavement. The pallid lights of the building on the upper level drew an approximate shadow across the lower level on which he stood alone. I knew this must be the funeral home.

I left the car and walked toward him in the quiet mode one deferentially and automatically assumes in these places. Each tread made me more aware of my leather soles stamping my progress on the damp tarmac.

"Am I alright to park here?" I asked in that way peculiar to men untrained in the niceties or needs for introductions.

"You are boy," he countered in a non-committal way, his soft Cork accent undulating easily on waves of his own making.

"Now if you want to park here," he continued as I turned away " we have a system."

He had my full attention. His greased white hair, a few weeks late for a cut, rubbed the raven collar of his overcoat. Raindrops from the last shower clustered on his patent shoes, light draining from them, reflecting darkness like the eyes of those who mourned the man inside. In the gathering darkness light from the streetlights found a place in his clear blue eyes as he took in my every movement.

I stood, maintaining what for me in company is always a difficult silence, leaving the door ajar for him to introduce me to the "system".

"Do you see that hearse over there?" I hadn't until then. It was parked in the exit preventing any novices to the protocol turning it into an entrance. Alongside it on the low wall was a large luminous exit sign. I wondered if anyone had commented on this irony, had any relative of someone recently departed felt hurt by this thoughtless pairing. I swallowed my natural inclination to comment.

"You pull up at right angles to it and as close to the wall as possible." I did as I was bid. I clicked the car shut and turned to my mentor. He seemed disinclined to elaborate further. I couldn't resist.

"So what's the system?"

"Ah that's aisy boy," he assured me. "Like most things in life but especially at funerals all you have to do is get the first fella right and the rest will follow."

We swapped smiles.

" Aren't I the lucky man that you turned up first and not some fella thinking he should be telling me what to do." With that our relativities were sealed. He was the boss. I silently relieved myself of the role that pertained to so much of my life.

"You're not from round here," he observed. I grasped his invitation to continue and heard myself filling in my 50 years in one breath.

"I'm a Tipp man via England to Galway."

"That's a long way to come to a funeral." he twinkled. "from Galway I mean," he added snuffing out any unintentional affront. "The poor man inside and his relations will be pleased with your effort."

"Tis the least I could do." I answered in the time honoured way as my eyes unnecessarily inspected my shoes. My mother's ambition for me to be educated and sorted in this life coupled with my five year sojourn with the De La Salle brothers trying to shape me for the next life had left me adept at dismissing praise under the baleful glare of duty.

I turned towards the hearse. I was early so there was a chance of getting a quick bite to eat in the orange lit pub on the corner opposite.

"I'll be seeing you," I said in an attempt to soften the parting.

"I hope it doesn't rain much before you get back," came the disjointed reply followed by a gap offering no further explanation.

"Why's that," I said jumping through the open trapdoor

"Because you've left the car window open on this side."

My laughter romped round the silent enclosure. "God you don't miss a trick do you," I answered and asked though gasps of frosty air.

"You can't in this line of work," he said with a gravity that grounded me in an attitude more suited to this solemn occasion. "Take the family of that poor man inside. They're in no state to be able to think of all the details. If I don't pay attention to the small things sure it just makes this whole thing all the harder for the poor devils. Now lock up your car and when you follow that man to the church you can come back and slip out nice and aisy." My education continued.

 "In fact the system is such that nobody can move until you do. There's no unions in this place," he smirked "You know. Last in first out"

He allowed himself a restrained laugh after a quick sweep over his shoulder to see that we were still two. The implicit warning about any delay on my part after the removal was not lost on me.

"Can I ask how you came in?"

"I came through the tunnel. I don't know my way through the city."

"You were right too," he agreed. I could give you directions but they would be a bit complicated."

"I got lost on the way in," I admitted, happy enough to reinforce his own view of my inability to follow complicated instructions.

He brought forward one hand and brushed something unseen from his shoulder. He dismissed the dandruff and my admission in one easy gesture.

"Ah you did not, sure otherwise we wouldn't be stood here talking. You were only temporarily astray."

I wondered if by some chance there was a God, this was the sort of assurance he should be giving to the penitent soul of the man laid inside.

"Now, the easiest way for you to find your way home." He paused. I waited expectantly.

" The easiest way is to do the reverse of what you did on the way in, except of course where you went astray."

The finality in the lilting voice told me it was time to leave him to prepare for the next part of his ritual. I ambled to the pub, his last pearl of wisdom nestling in the lines of my smile. How many people lost and unsure of their way home, unsure of how to undo the parts where they went astray would be comforted by his assurance that there was such a way.

I looked back. He had moved to a corner near the street and far from the hearse. The red glow of a cigarette framed his face.

We never swapped names. They're of little use in getting to know someone. Our names are other people's choices; given before they know us, born of their memories, hopes or family tradition. Men are unfortunate with name swapping. As soon as we do we follow up with "What do you do," and then the race is well and truly on to see who is the lead male in the pack.

In this Friday half-light our roles were crystal clear. He the funeral attendant, master of the system, keeper of the details, me the mourner, glad to be guided through the practicalities so I might harness my energy to deal respectfully with those who had lost a great deal more.

When you get to know who people are is time enough for them to have a name. We will never meet again. What we know about each other is as much as we will ever likely know maybe as much as we ought to know..

But I feel I should name him. I remember an old man growing up in my home place. He was poor, bedraggled and fond of the drink. He would sit at the corner of the street in an old wicker chair facing the bridge and the backdrop of the Knockmealdown Mountains. He played a badly tuned fiddle badly, the only way to do it I suppose. When I stopped crossing the road to pass him he stopped playing and spoke of wondrous things and places far away. His observations were at once acerbic but insightful. He was an intelligent man who had never travelled far to gain wisdom. He happily shared it with anyone willing to see behind the Guinness bottle glasses, the scarecrow hair and the three-patterned three-piece suit.

He was intelligent about fifty years too soon. His mother, abandoned early, must have known he was intelligent. In the midst of the Pats, Bills, Toms and other well-worn abbreviations she named him Cornelius.

So I shall name this man Cornelius. With such a name it is easy to remember that I was glad to meet him.

Dùag House

He woke with a start, taking a second to focus on the unfamiliar bedroom in his new home. The four of them had moved into the estate house by the river Dwagge a week before. Billy's father had left his Raleigh bicycle at work and brought home the forestry tractor and trailer that he drove across the mountains that were the backdrop to the small village in South Tipperary where he lived. Until now, the year after his Holy Communion he had lived in the Main Street opposite the old closed courthouse where his grandfather had his tailors shop until his death three years ago. The house was rented as few in the village could afford to buy their own. Out of the blue the landlord had served notice on his mother to quit.

His father had loaded and strapped their meagre possessions onto the trailer keeping an eye on the mountains for any signs of impending rain while neighbours kept watch from behind twitching net curtains. His mother had gone on ahead to their new home, Dwagge House, in order to dull the humiliation of being the object of charity by the one remaining English landlord Lord Sackville-West. This kindly man had heard about the family's plight and had offered them the use of an empty property on his estate, rent free, until they could get back on their feet.

Billy's younger brother stood in the cab with his father while he jumped in the trailer with his dog Toby. They followed the neglected track out of the village, the river on their right changing from still pools to mini rapids as it dropped over small weirs in its search for sea level. Two miles further on the track turned sharply between two moss covered pillars whose rusty brackets were the only hint at a gate that hadn't offered closed protection for many a year. The blue house, its paint peeling in large chunks, stood square and solid, it's panelled door set at the top of three large stone steps. Billy jumped off and raced across the semi-circle of gravel covering the width of the house dodging the thistles and nettles that had invaded from the nearby farmland. Toby chased behind barking and running in circles, confused by the space and the lack of customary admonishments to 'come here'.

He reached the top step as his mother swung open the door. 'Keep away from the upstairs' his mother reminded him 'We only have the use of the downstairs. The joists are not too good and I haven't found the key to lock it up as yet'

The two brothers spent the next week exploring their new home, the surrounding fields and of course the river. Many Cowboy and Indian fights took place. Ever present was the panting Toby. His mother scrubbed from dawn to dusk slowly rescuing the inside of the house from years of neglect while his father repelled the onward march of weeds and cleared the walled garden at the back in preparation for the sowing of potatoes and vegetables to help supplement the meagre buying power of his forestry worker wages.

Billy was fully awake now. His brother slept on in the bed pushed up against the other wall. Toby's whine was insistent and he was clawing something in the hall. Billy jumped out of bed, an involuntary intake of breath coinciding with the coldness of the uncovered wooden floor. He opened his bedroom door slowly to prevent the dry hinges from squeaking. The hall was lit only by moonlight pushing through the semi-circle of old stained glass above the front door, its lead fringed sections dissipating the light into shifting shadows on the faded plastered walls.

'Come here Toby'. No patter of pads greeted his whispered command. Toby stood at the door leading upstairs whining and scratching at the gap between jamb and door. Billy tiptoed down and grabbed him by the collar. Toby's whine changed to a low threatening growl and he stood rigid against Billy's pressure.

Billy let go. He was confused. He had Toby since he was a pup. He followed Billy everywhere, obeyed every command. Toby continued to scratch leaving his claw marks on the bare wood. Billy looked back down the hall checking for the telltale escaping triangle of light that would signal that one of his parents was awake. He twisted the stiff door knob to the forbidden upstairs. The door squeaked slowly from the frame. Toby nudged it wider with his snout and bounded upstairs. Billy followed carefully, looking for any holes or rotten timber on the stair treads. Each footstep was imprinted with a squeak. Billy reached the top without any call from downstairs. He stepped from the landing onto the hall. A few feet away Toby stood stock still outside a room from which emanated a bluish translucence that looked like no light Billy had ever seen. He felt the hairs on the back of his neck rise, his heart beat almost audibly within his ribcage.

He edged forward feeling his way down the wall to the room door which was slightly ajar. Swallowing repeatedly now as he tried to coax some saliva from his dry mouth he closed his eyes and pushed the heavy door with his hand. As the door started to swing soundlessly Toby yelped and headed downstairs. Billy's eyes shot open as he turned his head slowly, fearfully, to face into the room. The blue light filled the whole room but had no clear source. From ceiling to floor it seemed to shine equally. An old bed and wardrobe in one corner of the room cast no shadow. The light flex with a filthy bulb hung limply from the ceiling. Billy peered further round the frame to see the other half of the room. He stood transfixed, raw fear replacing apprehension. A figure stood near the large sash window that overlooked the front of the house where the river flowed. It was a young woman, at that stage somewhere between girl and woman. She was barefoot and dressed in a plain white nightdress that reached just below her knees. She was stooped forward holding the bottom of the window as if trying to open it. Her long fair hair fell forward obscuring her face. Billy stood motionless. Toby's slight whimpering from the safety of the landing seemed to curl round his feet. Slowly she turned. Her pale face looked as if she had been crying, yet there were no tears. As she fully faced him his eyes were drawn downwards. A large red patch that even Billy knew was blood coloured the pale nightdress from stomach to knees. She stood, knees together and bent, feet slightly splayed, a soundless pain escaping from her open mouth. Billy looked away but was immediately drawn back to the young girl. She had moved silently to the side of the bed in the corner furthest from the window. He had heard no movement, no squeaking floorboards, no rustle of clothing, and no disturbance of air. His lips parted and he exhaled without speaking. He knew there was no need. Her head moved rhythmically from his face to the window and back, a look of entreaty escaping from her frowning, pained blue green eyes. He knew without asking what he had to do. Despite the fear welling up inside he knew he had no choice. He moved forward slowly to the window. The hasp in the middle was open. He grasped the two faded brass handles on the bottom of the lower window frame and pulled upwards. To his surprise the sash moved easily upwards. The sound of the river was carried in on the cold night air causing him to gasp. The room was suddenly darker lit only by the pale light from the nearly full moon in the near cloudless sky. He turned back into the room. She was gone. He turned back to the window and leaned out. She was kneeling by the river, leaning inwards, reaching to retrieve something from the current. She stood up and turned round in the moonlight. She was holding a bundle close to her chest. She eased back the blanket to reveal a small blue petrified face. A sound like keening drifted upwards to Billy. She raised her head and her eyes fixed Billy's with a smile, filling him with a sudden calm. He blinked and she was gone. The night returned to being just the night. He closed the window and felt his way carefully across the room to the door. Now Toby went willingly with him down the stairs and along the hall to his blanket pile near the stove in the kitchen.

A week later and unable to put the girl from his mind Billy broached the subject with his mother. He asked her if there was some story about a girl having a baby in this house. His mother dropped the wooden spoon she had been using and turned on him.

"Where did you hear that," she demanded.

"Oh some of the bigger boys at school were saying that a girl had a baby without being married and that it had been taken from her and drowned."

His mother paled.

"You shouldn't be listening to rubbish like that. Now go to your room and get your homework done."

Billy turned away. He had heard adult whisperings about girls in trouble and how the local informal midwifes, a small number of local women, would sort out their troubles by taking the baby away, only to return soon after to inform the mother that the child had not survived. Billy also remembered that his mother was one of this small group.

He knew further enquiry was pointless.

Ground Swell

Elspeth had decided to go, despite what her father said. Robert was taking his boat out one last time before the summer ended. She picked her way across her bedroom floor, kicking her netball singlet into an already full corner. Anonymous love verses circled her mirror on multi coloured notelets. Her parents wouldn't see them. The latest maid she allowed in once a week didn't care. The large house was a series of compartments, rooms dedicated to people or functions. The only key to her bedroom pressed against her thigh as she sat down.

She had crouched to take one last look in the hall mirror. Her father liked to see her look her best. The framed memories in the drawing room tracked her growth from birth until now. Each a perfect pose, none of her hiding behind her mother's skirts during the many family parties, none caught unawares as she was paraded to relatives and friends, the sole evidence of her father's future hopes.

'Absolutely not. Haven't you heard about their firm? The fathers a gambler. He lowered his Washington Post.

She knew only to ask once. She gazed at him silently, pursed her lips and turned away. The expected change of heart was not forthcoming; the practised reaction that had won on so many occasions fell on deaf ears. She turned back. His grey hair crested the newspaper.

The bell hanging inside the rusted buoy clanged its mournful warning across the gentle rise and fall of the afternoon swell. Strewn across a blue sky, flimsy high clouds frayed at the edges, the telltale signs of high winds further out to sea. Robert's knuckles whitened as his grip on the tiller tightened. A glance from under his blue cap to the horizon showed him the yawning blue of a much deeper swell, one that would defy his single sail schooner.

She moved like a satiated cat to face him. Her scarlet smile seemed to tease, the swell of her breasts capturing his eyes, stoking his frustrated desire. It had been like this all summer.

Her lithe form gracing the small deck while the three young male friends vied for drops of attention dispensed without pattern, without predictability from the largesse of her self awareness, her sensuous grace in his imaginings matched only by his boat as it caressed and penetrated the waves. She had stopped showing any interest in him some weeks ago; avoiding him in the isolated places they had previously shared. The salty spray cast memories of the taste of her skin. Her whispered promises, the memory of their snatched nights together in the boat shed came again with the usual stomach tightening anger.

"Should we not go back? We're at the buoy." Elspeth sought assurance from Jack who was studiously ignoring her.

"You mean come about don't you?" The testiness of Jacks reply attracted Benjamin and Lucas, posing bare chested for her benefit and their suntan.

"Last week of the vacation. Let's go out further. Test this little beauty. We'll be locked away in college soon. What do you say guys. Men or boys."

By now she was ignoring him, rearranging herself to drink in the late summer sun.

The boys looked at each other nervously. In his planning he had gambled that they wouldn't wish to exhibit any weakness in front of her. The gamble paid off.

It had all happened so quickly. His mother had told him through her wet lace handkerchief of the failure of the family business, his father's business, the three generation descriptor of who they were in the tight, exclusive Newport, Rhode Island community. The business, during the post war recession, was unable to dance to the tempo of his father's gambling addiction. The threat of repossession of all their material monuments of respect spread faster than a rumour that a black man was looking to move in. And then his mother was gone as she had arrived, powerless, without a say, rescued from the ignominy by her ever vigilant family.

"Cutting our losses," the white bearded patriarch explained without emotion. Jack wasn't invited to come. He must be one of their losses. The acceptance to the university that his family always went to was withdrawn; an apology for an administrative error a poor cloak for his regrading outside the only normality he knew. Jack couldn't tell anyone, wouldn't tell anyone. He floated rudderless for three months at the mercy of the tides of pretence.

And now he had been told that his boat was to be reclaimed. This cherished gift that had marked his transition to manhood. The one place where he was master; where he was better than his father. Always at home on the water, that dimension between this world and eternity. The last pillar of control in his life was crumbling in the storm force winds of changes that he could not control, that no one he had previously relied on could control. He was an observer silently screaming as his previous existence and promised future disintegrated.

He found a new focus, a meaning in his decision to end the rip tide of her rejection; that final onslaught on the crumbling shoreline of what remained of his life. He had left the lifejackets and emergency flares in the boat shed. He had left no note. He knew an invite to his two friends would bring her. He regretted that. He eased the tiller away swinging the white sail round to tack into the rising wind, heading for the deeper blue, a ground swell of calm rising within him.

In life you never know

His eyes opened slowly to the familiars in the bedroom. He felt tired. His brothers bed, the West Ham pictures round his own corner of the room, the quartered skylight showing the drops of another shower arriving from the nearby mountains, the cheap curtain covering the under stairs storage area all swam in and out of view, in and out of his concentration. His thoughts flitted in and out on his flicking eyelids, needing to be repeated to be held onto. He found it difficult to fill in the blacked out gaps in this jumping film.

Something was wrong, shapes and noises out of place, too many voices in this place, in his space within the family home. He went to rise, barely noticing he was fully dressed, not trying to interpret the cause of the blood stained pillow.

That was it!

"What are you two doing up here".

His two best friends, Bas and Fred stood at the end of the bed.

"You collapsed in Lawlor's arch before Mass. We brought you home". Bas explained. Fred nodded to confirm any doubt.

Lawlor's arch was attached to their current drinking hole. It had a small door set in the large wooden arched doors. It was never locked. It doubled as an entrance for underage drinkers who couldn't be seen going in the main door and as a bolt hole from raids by the Garda who by some unwritten but understood protocol always came in the front door. They were the days before computer analysed statistics when the number of raids undertaken was sufficient to satisfy the powers above. The number of people not prosecuted as a result of these efforts was impressive. The pub faced across the wide main street to the high steepled village church in defiance of any sermons that might be delivered on the evils of drink. The doors of both establishments synchronised for all the major occurrences in the village, births, marriages deaths and hurling matches. Billy and his friends met there before the ritual Sunday Mass to make sure they got a pillar at the back to lean against. In their journey away from religion and towards manhood they had given up frequenting the pews which they saw as the domains of the old who were enslaved in their devotion and the very young who as yet had no choice in the matter. The back pillars of the body of the church and the vestibule with its large semi-circular stone Holy water fonts was where the work of re conversion could have commenced. Instead the parish priest was content to measure the strength of faith by counting the contents of the collection plates.

"It must have been all that vodka you drank last night after you two winning the darts tournament" Fred smirked. Billy's mother, who until now he hadn't noticed, or had he, threw a baleful look that caused the smirk to be replaced by an anxious cough which kept time with Fred's shuffling feet.

'It's no joke' she said. "Falling down like that in front of the whole village. As if this place hasn't had enough trouble with drink down the years without you lot starting down the same road"

"Are you all right now missus" asked Bas. They hadn't got to the stage yet where they would use her first name. They hadn't been given permission. They would have a few more vodkas drank before that would happen. Billy answered, sensing their desire to leave

"I'm alright lads. I just want to sleep. I'll see ye tonight".

They took the offered escape and both being tall lads, ran head and shoulders down the steep one way stairs that led to the main room of the house which took them straight onto the street and away from the congestion of the small upstairs room.

"With the cut of you, you won't be going anywhere tonight." His mother wrinkled her lip, shook her head with the disdain of a tee totaller who had seen the effects of drink in her husband's family and disappeared downstairs. Through the thin ceiling he could hear snippets of her sermon being thrust unbidden on to the man of the house who was known to like a pint or several as an escape from many aspects of his life.

He reached for the packet of Majors that were thrown in the tin ashtray on the bedside chair. He jerked, knocking the lot on the lino floor, thought better about feeding this other addiction, turned into the soft bolster pillow and fell asleep.

Three years later things were much different. He had swapped the small village nestling under the Knockmealdown Mountains in South Tipperary for a Nurses home in a hospital for the intellectually disabled in the rolling countryside of Kent in South East England. The certainties, the one accent, the immutable rules and relativities of the four hundred odd people joined by long presence and intermarriage had been forsaken on a whim of self-discovery. There were more people in his new home, the Nurses home, than in the whole village. The patients all belonged to one family, one label, the mentally subnormal. This new society had accents that had to be located in the world's geography. Relativities were on the power relationship between nurse and patient and within the nurse family. He was now the junior represented by the grey epaulet on his white coat; the nursing assistant. Combination drinks such as light and bitter, brown and mild challenged the previous world of Guinness and Smithwicks. He still wondered how anyone could drink flat ales with names like Bishops finger.

So here he was on his first day on the wards of this institution when one of the patients crashed to the floor causing an almost complete non reaction from other patients and a practiced response from the other staff. He stood in the splendid isolation and inertia of one who doesn't know what to do. The excitement waned and the young man was taken on unsteady feet up to the dormitory he shared with thirty other inmates.

"What happened?" he embarrassingly enquired of a passing qualified nurse.

"He had a blackout, you know a fit." He imparted this knowledge without breaking stride on his way back to the office to write up the shift report.

Billy froze; the words blackout and fit chasing each other round his brain, reaching out to span his attempts at keeping them unconnected. He recalled the two or three other blackouts before leaving on this journey of self-discovery, usually after a particularly heavy night on the town. But given that he and his friends were out every night of the weekend and if they could afford it during the week he had come to accept it as inevitable that there would be one or two spattered here and there. The worst that had ever happened to him was a large bump on the head which made his straight shoulder length hair hard to wash and comb for a few days after.

The passing nurse's explanation had just dropped a bombshell of inestimable proportion onto the assuredness of his life. He thought he knew who he was. There was evidence of who he was all round him in the village and town lands of his erstwhile home. The graveyard embraced by the nearby mountain and serenaded by the gentle river was littered with the leaning stone rolls of his ancestry. He was good at school because that was what was required. He was a good footballer probably again because that was what was required if you took it up seriously. Old Tobin the great GAA thinker and equally good whiskey drinker had told his father that it was a "crying shame" he was taking the road to England. His father explained sadly that scoring goals and points for Clogheen wouldn't put food on the table. They nodded knowingly.

Now he stood in the middle of the dayroom of what were ironically called villas with the bored patients wandering aimlessly round the space and the words and their implications racing round his lack of information.

Blackouts are fits. Fits are another word for epilepsy. All the people here who have epilepsy are mentally subnormal. Is there a link between the two? Have I got the same thing? Will I become like them? The thoughts seemed disembodied as if shouted at him by others. He had been in England for three months. He wasn't sure if he had any blackouts since his arrival. He remembered, almost unwillingly, waking in his small room in the nurses home feeling exhausted after a night's sleep. On one occasion his tongue was cut and swollen on one side making it feel about two sizes too big for his mouth. He spent two days trying to manoeuvre it around cornflakes and words over which he now seemed no longer to be master. Could that have been one? The immensity of his thoughts, the implication for him of the only logical conclusion that could be drawn from them swamped him like an unexpected large wave in the rhythm of an incoming tide. He had secured his place on a training course to be a nurse. The school was due to start in three month's time. He had ended the predictable, almost expected cycle of going to work and then the pub in the unchanging environment that had allowed little change of note in successive generations of its inhabitants. The adage that the only news was local news no longer applied to his life. The people he now lived amongst were not interested in who his father was and what he did. He was judged by who he was. What he could achieve was, in the main, up to him and not a set of unwritten rules of an intransigent structure. He would no longer have to walk out of the village alone to date the daughter of those who considered themselves well to do. The expectations on him were his own, not the limiting ones of his family's understanding of 'their place'.

And now this dawning realisation that another tag might be ascribed to and define his life. He did what most would do in his place. He denied it. It couldn't be the same as these people he was caring for. Anyway it wasn't serious enough to mention.

A year later his girlfriend woke to a commotion on the other side of the bed in her room in the ground floor flat she shared with a friend. Her new boyfriend was thrashing violently, legs and arms flailing at all sorts of unpredictable angles. She switched on the bedside light. His breathing was laboured, his lips blue. A squirt of something warm hit her legs. As she turned him on his side the convulsing stopped and he seemed to wake. He was trying to get out of bed. She begged him to stay where he was. He didn't seem to recognise her; asking who she was and where he was. He pushed her away when she tried to hold him. She sat in the old wicker chair in the corner of the room and waited until he dropped into a deep, snoring sleep. Even though she was a trainee nurse, she was frightened.

The next day he awoke feeling like someone who had been on a tiring but refreshing workout, gasping, as his father used to say, with the drought and famished. While he replenished his bodily needs she took him through, in detail, what unconsciousness had saved him of being aware. He agreed to see a doctor.

The consulting room was at the end of a long drab corridor whose walls were surrendering its coats of off white paint to the vagaries of time and the demands of gravity. As he watched the hanging peels he was reminded that the hospitals first use eight hundred years ago was a leper colony.

A round faced nurse called his name, handed him a file with his name on and pointed him without further instruction to the only door behind her desk. As he entered he saw the balding patch escaping the full head of grey hair that hid the face of the consultant poring over someone else's file.

"Sit down."

Everything in the room looked old. The faded leather cover on the desk curled where the brass retaining studs had gone missing. Black shapes on the walls of absent pictures suggested an intention to redecorate that was never achieved. The strip lights in the ceiling seemed to be losing the battle with shadows that encroached from each corner. A permeating smell of damp reinforced the recent headlines in the local paper of plans for closure and centralization of services. This general decay extended to the one empty chair which made his choice of where to sit very manageable. He gave the seat a peremptory flick with his hand. The man in the jumbled coat with the jumbled hair looked up from the jumble of paper. His clear blue eyes drew Billy back from the room inspection to the purpose of the consultation. Although Billy sensed he was aware of his appraisal of his work area no comment was offered or invited. Billy thought, with some anxiety, how well he suited the room.

"It looks like you have got epilepsy ……… William" he added after consulting the front of the drab brown file.

"It's Billy." He couldn't know that both Billy and his grandfather had never used their given name except in an official capacity, in other words when requested by people who understood themselves to be in the position of authority. Billy would always remember the first bank account he opened in his used name. He had stepped out from the yoke of fixed expectations.

"Well Billy," he emphasized in his Home Counties accent "if you are here looking for me to cure you of this affliction then you may as well leave now and save you and me a great deal of our valuable time."

Billy reached back for the jacket draped on the back of the chair.

The consultant ignored the reaction to his opening rejoinder and continued moving the plum round his fleshy mouth.

"However if you wish me to help you to get it under control and live a normal life then we can possibly do some business."

Billy thought of the recent description of his latest 'blackout' given by his girlfriend. There was no other game in town. He sat back down, noting the slight smile that passed across the wrinkled face across the desk. He wondered how many times this opening had been used with the same effect.

"How did you get on," asked his girlfriend as she sat down in her white uniform, her shoeless feet on the footstool with her cup of hot chocolate after the miles walked on the late shift on her current placement on a medical ward.

Billy could only remember two specific things apart from the usual listing of tests to come. His new mentor in this major addendum to his life had asked him if he knew who Roger Bannister was. Given Billy's obvious Irish accent but not being aware of his natural propensity to become interested in most sports he was duly impressed with his prompt answer. His mother said that if the telly broke down during a match he would watch two flies walk across the ceiling.

"Well having a typical seizure, a grand mal is like running the sub four minute mile in about thirty seconds. Just because you wake up doesn't mean you will feel able to jump up and take on the world. You have to give yourself time to recover. Let your body tell you not the other way around."

Blackout as a term fell far short as an adequate description for this type of occurrence. He dropped it from that day.

The second point was the most important. Taking it on board meant he was able to go forward in his life, in his dreams with this affliction put firmly in its place.

"Now young man." He peered over his pince nez spectacles in an avuncular expression of empathy that had survived his constant exposure to the afflicted;

"It's my job to treat the epilepsy. And I'm reasonably good at it. It's your job to take my advice. I hope you are reasonably good at that. If we both do our bit then we have a reasonable chance of getting this condition under reasonable control That's all I can promise you. If I could cure you I wouldn't have to sit in this hell hole every day."

Billy smiled at the confirmation that his initial room scan had been observed and nodded in expected agreement of the mutual roles within the burgeoning relationship.

"But the greatest task you have in relation to your condition I regret I can't help you with."

Billy sat upright, his blue eyes focused unblinking on the other.

"If you want to pursue whatever dreams, and I mean the waking ones, that you have then you will have to do your damnedest not to become an epileptic."

Billy frowned having already become proficient in its use to describe patients he worked with in the hospital.

"You can make a profession out of it, let it be how the world sees you or you can live with it and dominate it. Your choice young man. I have no tests or tablets that can help you. And between you and me I'm not a great fan of psychologists. Have a look at this list." He rummaged in the top drawer of the desk displacing some of its contents to start another pile on the surrounding floor.

Billy took the wrinkled photocopy headed 'Famous people who had epilepsy'. He skimmed the list, Van Gogh, Joan of Arc, Napoleon, Socrates, Byron, Nobel, and Saint Paul.

"Now, if you were describing any of these would you describe them as epileptics?"

Billy smiled as he folded the list with his prescription. He didn't need to answer.

Some veils fell from his eyes that day. He added epilepsy to the list of things that could describe his totality. He stopped denying the reality and jettisoned the safe tag of blackouts. He found a place for epilepsy in his life that left him intact and only slightly damaged. Epileptic became for him a hated term which he would take every opportunity to resist in relation to all people with epilepsy.

Secretly he wondered if the condition had made any contribution to the greatness of the list folded inside his prescription.

In life you never know.

Maltkiln House

The door of the pub made tall men enter with humility. He reached for the black iron handle set in the dark brown wood. A flash of red from above darted into the edge of his vision. A grey plaque, embedded in the yellowing plaster betrayed the building's functional past 'Maltkiln House 1749.' In those days local hostelries brewed their own beer, real ale. Above the plaque was the source of the colour, a painted phoenix, newer, incongruous, staring outwards with ever spread wings, threatening to but never being able to leave.

His gaze drifted to the larger building next door. It stood like a guardian, casting its shadow through the soft evening light, a brooding sentinel overseeing its smaller charge. He walked slowly past its solid, unremarkable façade to its one gable end. A wooden platform jutted out from two doors set high on the gable. The wood was streaked black with signs of an old fire. Above the door in the shadow of the inverted v a pulley wheel was set in the wall, rusted, redundant. He imagined the workers, arms straining from the sleeves of their collarless shirts, their hobnailed boots gaining purchase on the platform as they pulled the large sacks of rye hops from the horse drawn drays below.

His reverie was interrupted as his eyes dropped to a place on the gable just out of reach of a tall man. A russet plaster face stared out from the wall in the direction of the church spire pointing heavenwards above a line of sycamores bordering the village green. The profile needed no name, the goatee beard , the horns were clearly those of the demon, the instantly recognisable visage of evil, the custodian of man's falling, humanity's damnation. Below the face three rows of six concave circles of glass sat in the wall. Despite the sunlight flickering through the trees no light bounced from the glass. To him it seemed as if the light was being sucked into and beyond the glass. He stepped closer to the wall. The breeze seemed to halt, not drop, just halt. Behind him the trees still tried to shake loose their dying leaves, the uncut grass verges swayed with each gust. But close to the wall stillness held sway, not the balmy quiet of a summers day, not the heavy calm before a storm. This was a wall behind which sounds, smells, vital things had no place. He moved away. The wind ruffled his hair, putting him at ease. High up the face looked outward, challenging, and expectant. He returned to the front of the building and headed once more to the door. A movement caught his eye. A young man's face peered out from one of the six windows on the first floor. Even in the dimming evening light his expression conveyed a distraught troubled look. The unblinking eyes seemed to be seeking or seeing something beyond the normal range of vision. He halted; the head above him moved and then receded back into the unlit room. He shook his head, silencing his too rich imagination.

The black handle of the door turned easily as he stepped into the low ceilinged bar. The clicking of the latch seemed to prompt the half dozen customers to turn their heads in unison. Silently they registered the stranger in their midst and reverted back to their murmuring conversation. The barman sat on a high stool at one end of the bar. His tousled white hair crept over his ears and draped carelessly towards his sprouting eyebrows which harboured the last of his original brown hair. He cast an idle glance towards the stranger but not long enough to distract him from the crossword in the four times folded newspaper lying in front of him on the counter.

"Do you have rooms to rent," the new arrival enquired.

"We have a few." The answer came from the mouth hidden by the inclined head. "Bed only mind you, stopped doing food years ago when the wife died. Not much call for it round here these days," The soft Lancashire accent faded to silence.

"I'll take a room for two nights then."

The old man reached behind him to a small cabinet on the wall next to a display of roasted peanuts and pork scratchings. He slid a key with a plastic tag across the counter.

"Number 4 at the front of the house. I'm in number six. Bathroom and toilet are across the corridor. The front door is locked at half twelve each night."

Without another word he eased himself with a slight wince from the stool to answer the silent request of one of his customers waving an empty glass. The swish of the hand pumped ale hit the glass as the stranger turned towards the stairs.

The room was small. A black metal framed bed stood in one corner. No quilts here. A number of blankets laid on of crisp white sheets. On top was a crocheted harlequin assortment of squares that came together as a bedspread. The bedsprings creaked as he slung his knapsack on top and sat down. A chunky wardrobe with a black flecked mirror, a three drawer dressing table with lace doilies and a low creased leather armchair swallowed up most of the remaining floor space. The one cast iron radiator under the window grumbled as if to assure him that the heating was on. Above it eight small lead lined window panes set in a deep recess overlooked the centre of the village. He unlaced and pulled off his walking boots and peeled off his slightly smelly woollen socks. His feet stretched into their new found freedom. He had been hiking round Lancashire for two weeks, sticking to the narrow country roads that linked old villages strewn between the motorway arteries that ferried thousands by each day. These small parish clusters pulsed to a more considered beat than the headlong rush of humanity nearby. This was the final stop before he returned to his life as a psychiatric nurse across the spine of the Pennines in Leeds. This was his release each year; to pick out the quiet places of his adopted country, to walk them alone. The old ornate metal sign in the middle of the little roundabout told strangers they were in Little Eccleston. Locals had known for generations. Whitewashed stones marked the green central circle, its flower beds past their summer best. Two and three story buildings sat on the edge of flagged paths, their ground floors dressed in red brick, their overhanging upper stories showing their original timber frames in black beams that traversed fading uneven plaster. The circle of houses was broken to allow three roads to head off like streams wending their way to a faraway river.

As he undid the ties on his green knapsack a moan came from the room next door. He could just discern the creaking of floorboards. He moved to the dividing wall and closed his eyes in concentration. The moaning was a man's voice. He could distinguish no words. Suddenly a shout echoed down the hall. "Be Quiet." The sound from the room next door ceased, footsteps faded from the corridor and the silence was broken only by the chuntering of the heating system. His natural curiosity guided him to pick out his wash things and head down the corridor to the bathroom. Maybe the moaner would show himself. As he reached the end of the corridor he noted the brass number 6 screwed to the landlord's bedroom door. He turned towards the bathroom and looked at the number 4 on his room key tag. He turned back and walked slowly back down the corridor towards the stairs. There was no room with the number 5. The bathroom was cold. The cast iron bath stood in the middle. As the warming water tumbled from the brass tap a mist formed on the dark green tiles and off white grout gradually merging to form mini rivulets that ran to the heavy floorboards. He shaved quickly. He liked to shave in the evenings on these trips, breaking the ritual of the usual early morning preparation for the workday. He dumped his socks pants and shirt to soak in the sink and jumped into the bath. The warm water wrapped round him as he laid back, every muscle responding to the gentle massage. The scream made him jump up causing a tide back and forth in the bath that washed over the sides.

"He's coming back again. Get rid of him. You didn't believe me. I'm afraid. Please. Please. Do something." The words were replaced by screaming.

"Get back in your room. Get hold of him. Grab him before he tries to go downstairs."

The scuffle on the landing reached the bathroom door causing it to shake in its frame. A door was opened and then slammed. The screaming faded but continued. By now he was standing in the middle of the room holding the coarse bath towel, unable to understand what had just happened. He had no doubt that the screams came from the face he had seen earlier at the first floor window and was the person in the room with no number. He towelled himself quickly, rinsed his laundry and opened the bathroom door. The landlord and a younger thickset man passed him.

"Is everything alright? What was the screaming about?"

"Nowt for you to worry about lad."

Without further explanation they disappeared down the stairs at the end of the hall.

Half an hour later he entered the tap room. He preferred these public bars. This was where to meet the regulars, the local characters. While they might look you up and down the stranger's willingness to be among them encouraged their natural curiosity and hospitality. Plus there was always the chance for them of a free pint from a flush visitor. The bar was dominated by a pool table. Its fading green cloth bore evidence of rough use. On another wall a dartboard, its wire rising slightly from the outer ring hung underneath a garish wall light. A roughly painted white line on the floor marked the throwing distance. Fading pictures of darts and pool teams with long gone trophies decorated the window wall. A motley assortment of round tables and wooden stools lined the walls. Along the window wall a long seat with leather seat and a carved wooden back evidenced an earlier period.

"Are you staying above?" The question came from a lean framed man nursing the dregs of a flat pint."

"Just a couple of days before I head back to work."

"A couple of days here is enough for anyone."

"What do you mean?"

"You must have heard the row above earlier."

I did. What was it all about?"

"That was the landlord's nephew making the row. Very sad situation. He came to live her as a young fella. His parents were killed in a car crash on the M62. Went under a French articulated lorry one night during a snowstorm. About nine years ago he became convinced that the door on the gable end of this place was a portal to the underworld and that the devil was getting access to this world and was responsible for attacks on young women.

"Was that the door with burn marks I saw earlier?"

"That's it. The burn marks are left over from the night that the young lad tried to burn it down. He was convinced it was the only way to get rid of this curse. Did a fair bit of damage. Cost his uncle a mint to put it back in working order. That's what the phoenix is about out the front. The uncle put it up as a sort of weird reminder of that time. The young fella got worse and worse. In the end he stopped going out. Stayed in his room watching out for the devil. He started taking his meals in his room. When he got really bad he went screaming through the village. Grabbed a couple of young girls once on their way home from school and tried to force them into the church for safety. That was as much as the village could take. The uncle was threatened that the young lad would be taken away and be locked up."

"But he is still here."

"That was four years ago. His uncle closed up the door leading from the lad's room and knocked out one to his own room. That door stays locked most of the time. Sometimes the young lad makes a break for it, like tonight."

"So that's why there's no number 5 above. The poor bugger lives in that one room."

"It's better than being locked up in some mental asylum. Your man inside would do anything to prevent that, given what happened to his brother and his wife. He vowed to look after the lad as if he was his own. I had better be heading off or her indoors will be looking for me. " He drained the last of his pint, turned up his jacket collar and headed out through the lounge bar.

He was now alone in the tap room. He picked his pint up and walked through to the more comfortable lounge bar. A smattering of customers occupied some of the bar stools and tables. He chose a seat near the wide open fire that gave him a good view of the bar. Locals gave him a cursory glance or nod. No one attempted a conversation.

The pub door sucked warm air out of the bar and smoke back down the chimney. The traveller looked round, like a local, to note the new entrant. The man entering drew himself to his not inconsiderable height. His dark eyes did a sweep of the room and its occupants. Conversations dribbled to silence as he commanded full attention. Raindrops on his brightly polished shoes picked up the flickering firelight. He slowly took off a long dress coat and old fashioned hat and hung them on the coat stand near the door. He placed an ornate topped cane into the umbrella stand. The owner jumped down from his place at the corner of the bar and disappeared into the kitchen area. The newcomer turned and strode slowly to a table where the ceiling lights struggled to cast their light. Two couples at nearby tables moved away almost in unison. The newcomer sat erect, black gloved hands palm downwards on the wooden table. The traveller at the fireside glanced sideways at the newcomer, not knowing why he had a feeling that he should not examine him directly.

The owner reappeared with a tray laden with steaming food dishes. His more usual gruff manner was replaced by an eyes down, obsequious attitude as he wiped the table and presented the newcomer with the food. The traveller grabbed him as he passed.

"I thought you said you didn't do food. Who's your man that he gets treated differently?"

"Not now lad. You only need to know as much as you ought to." He disengaged his arm from the travellers grip and returned to his stool behind the bar. Knowing glances but no words passed between the regulars at the bar. It seemed to the traveller that everyone was studiously trying to avoid contact with the newcomer. He was also sure that this newcomer was no stranger. Small communities place close attention to strangers until they can fit them into their social order. They only ignore those they know. He wondered why this newcomer evoked such regard. He instinctively knew there was probably no point in asking anyone.

The newcomer ate slowly, deliberately, seeming to savour each mouthful. Having finished he dabbed attentively at his closely clipped moustache and goatee beard. He folded the linen napkin, placed it beside the empty plate and carefully put on his gloves. He moved easily to the door, unmoved by all the eyes watching his progress, put on his coat and hat, picked up his cane and, head bowed, left the bar. The door latch clinked as he pulled it behind him. A collective exhaling from the customers marked his exit. The newcomer had spoken to no one but had affected everyone. Whispers and head nodding maintained the tense atmosphere after he had left.

The traveller finished his pint and went upstairs. He needed a good night's sleep before he caught the morning bus back to Leeds and the return to his work life. He slept fitfully, waking to thoughts of the newcomer and the ramblings of the young man in the sealed room next door. A feeling of frustration at something incomplete, unexplained underpinned his thoughts.

As he stood at the bar nest morning settling his account with the owner a loud knocking on the still locked pub door made both of them jump. The owner shot back the heavy black bolts and opened the door.

"Good morning Sergeant. Is there a problem? The young fella upstairs hasn't been screaming again has he?"

"If it was only that simple Mike." The policeman stepped across the threshold.

"We're putting together a search party and we're looking for all the men to give us a hand. It's the caravan park up the road. A seventeen year old girl is missing. She hasn't been seen since about ten last night. I hear you had a visitor here last night"

"Enough about that for now. I'll get my jacket. I hoped I would never have to do this again. Wait a minute while I make sure your man upstairs is locked in." The traveller stepped in front of him as he crossed to the stairs.

"What's going on? Do you need a hand?"

"No lad. It's best if you get that bus as planned and keep well away from things you don't understand. You don't want to get dragged into the curse that covers this place. Enough of us are trapped and damned by it."

As he waited alone at the bus stop he glanced back at Maltkiln house. The face at the upstairs window stared unblinking over the square, unaware of the traveller watching.

Official Collector

Joe had barely noticed her on his way in to the bank. Just another charity worker. Joe was in a hurry, squeezing a few tasks into his lunch hour. Most people hurry into banks as if each transaction is afforded a window of opportunity that must not be missed; as if hurrying will somehow get you to the top of the queue quicker. Joe always queued. If a mistake was to be made then he wanted to know who did it. He resisted the offer of placing cheques in envelopes and leaving them to be dealt with by some faceless employee in the back office. The recently offered internet banking facility communication had received only a cursory glance before being filed in the recycling bin.

'Rare is the person who can weigh the faults of others without putting his thumb on the scales' Lord Byron.

He didn't notice her because he had got used to people standing or sitting outside banks and shops in luminous vests or sashes rattling their requests for him to supplement the shortfalls in his monthly tax donation. He had become adept at walking with his head down, unwilling to face the silent assertion that he had disposable income that should go to yet another deserving cause. For him the rattling tins had fallen silent, the explanatory cards wiped of information, the outstretched hands paralysed as he excused himself of any responsibility for the difficulties of others.

"If you give to one you have to give to all. So I don't give to any," Joe would explain if the subject came up for discussion in the unchallenging company of his pay as you earn friends.

"It's demeaning to live on charity," he would assert without any experience.

What stopped him on the way out of the bank was the shaking. She was parked in a chipped grey wheelchair festooned with peeling stickers of a previous Manchester United team. She was far enough from the bank door to allow smooth escape for customers but barely far enough from the footpath edge to escape the shifting line of the shuffling taxi rank. Her fingers, red from the cold, protruded from fingerless gloves that rested on the table tray. The space between tray and chair back kept her somewhat upright, but couldn't prevent her head being bowed forward in an attitude of supplication that seemed to fit her situation. A silent mist was slipping up from the seafront, settling on her clothes and hair. She was twitching, stopping, jerking, stopping, fingers flicking like a baton less conductor negotiating an unfamiliar score, her muscles reacting to her own internal score. Thick lensed glasses with Elastoplast reinforcements swung precariously from one ear that poked out from under her red and white hat; the uneven stripes testifying to a poor home knitted imitation of what was on sale at the Old Trafford gift shop. Her heavy wool coat bulged through the restrictions of an undersized yellow Official Collector vest. This compulsory garment separated her from equally needy unofficial Collectors and other exponents of socially unacceptable begging. Strewn around the path were the collar pins that proved you had already given, that allowed you to deal face to face with repeated requests from other strategically positioned Official

Collectors and of course always looked well on the collar. Charity always assumes extra value when displayed.

'One may have a blazing hearth in one's soul and no one comes to sit by it. Passers-by see only a wisp of smoke from the chimney and continue on their way'. Vincent Van Gogh.

The donation tin with its untrusting sealed lid lay at the feet of a young man using the ATM machine. He was concentrating on the sun paled information on the screen and in not coming face to face with the collector. He certainly seemed unaware of the drama unfolding behind him. Without his glasses Joe could only see one word on the now unnecessary poster that dangled from the two strips of red electrical tape on the front of the tray: EPILEPSY. He folded his money into his wallet and pushed past two women who stood watching, nodding their heads from a safe distance. He ran his finger round the inside of his collar touching the heat of his rising temper.

The card enclosed in plastic that hung round her neck from the red and white string held all the information one would require about a non person.

'My name is Maria. I am an epileptic. If I require help please ring; and there followed two numbers, one a landline and one a mobile phone. Joe decided that it was more appropriate to call an ambulance. He conscripted one of the women onlookers to perform the task. She immediately jumped over the invisible line that separates onlookers from interveners and took the offered mobile phone with a smile on her face. People are only too happy to help. They only need to be asked and, of course, to feel that someone else is in charge.

'No one is useless in the world who lightens the burden of another' Charles Dickens.

Joe released the one brake on the wheelchair that worked and pushed Maria into the bank past a confused and momentarily objecting queue at the Foreign exchange counter. He offered the Customer help desk the opportunity to implement all those much vaunted claims about being the caring bank. His well-practiced grumpy expression offered only one acceptable answer to his request.

'Life's too short for chess' Lord Byron.

They managed to get him a room without even asking if Maria was one of their customers. The manager, who by now had arrived to assess this unusual transaction being processed in his otherwise organized environment, took one look at Joe talking to Maria's convulsing frame and diagnosed that tea for all was required.

'Society is now one polished horde, the bores and the bored'
Lord Byron.

The blond customer service staff checking her split ends in the safety of the doorway offered to do the necessary. With a sheepish grin towards Joe and an authoritative wave of his hand to his employee the manager insisted on attending to it personally. Nothing like walking the job to know what's really going on.

By now flashes of consciousness were sparking through the seizure. Maria's blissful unawareness of her situation was crumbling. She scrabbled over the sides of the wheelchair for the tin while her limbs continued to dance to the disordered signals from her brain. To anyone passing and glancing in it might have seemed as if she was trying to beat off an attempted robbery by this man in his wholly respectable suit.

Joe's foot slipped as he moved to prevent her head from banging on the handles of the chair. The floor was wet and the pungent smell of strong urine was suffusing the small interview room. Maria started to undo her coat and make efforts to get up from the chair. Joe eased her back gently. The message to use the toilet had come too late. Joe grabbed a sheaf of handouts on financial investment opportunities from the desk to arrest the puddle and threw open the window. He could do little to minimize the embarrassment that Maria was slowly experiencing in the lucid gaps.

'I must lose myself in action lest I wither in despair' Moliere.

Despite his best efforts Joe still knew no more about her than was on the plastic card in his inside pocket. By the time the ambulance came Maria's activity had reduced to transient absences that lasted just long enough for her to lose the thread of any conversation Joe was trying to have with her. Her fingers and lower legs flicked out the dying steps of her neuron fueled dance.

'I had a dream which was not all a dream' Lord Byron

"Ah Maria I thought it might be you." The ambulance man greeted his former customer. Maria flicked a brief smile of recognition. As he wheeled her to the ambulance, in his colour matched reflective coat, Joe added emergency personnel to the wider family of Official Collectors.

Joe sat alone in the interview room looking at the identity card. He was fuming, turning it over and over in his hands. 'I am an epileptic' screamed through the wrinkled heat sealed plastic cover. This summary of Maria's being, this defining characteristic, this sum of her existence captured in this all encompassing label. Her common forename would be easily forgotten but that tag would be emblazoned on the memory of anyone reading it. Another member of yet another group tossed outside the Pale of smug normality.

'Glory is fleeting but obscurity is forever.' *Napoleon Bonaparte.*

His eyes flicked momentarily. His hands gripped the chair sides. His thigh muscles tightened without his conscious prompt. He recognized the signs. The previous bad night's sleep and now getting stressed were not a good combination for someone who had epilepsy since he was eighteen. In the intervening thirty two years he had managed to have epilepsy without becoming an epileptic. Epilepsy was just part of who he was not who he was. He crumpled the card in his tight fist, locking in his indignation. He left the room, almost calm once more.

'If one sticks too rigidly to ones principles one would hardly see anybody' Agatha Christie.

As he passed the customer service desk he slid the tag to the girl who had helped him. He asked her to ring the contact numbers. She nodded and smiled and quietly accepted the responsibility.

'Ability is nothing without opportunity' Napoleon Bonaparte.

He stepped onto the wet footpath. The collectors tin had gone.

"Miserable bastards." he said aloud; adding another quote to those more famous people who also had epilepsy but had never become epileptics.

Nobody heard him.

The Thimble

He pulled the stool up to the bar of the little one room pub conveniently located next door to the bed and breakfast that was to be his home for the next six days. Outside the murky windows a light mist was slowly covering the mountains that would be his workplace during his stay. When he eagerly volunteered to do a first geological field trip he had visions of returning each day to his bachelor pad in his native Dublin. Being dispatched to this small village in South Tipperary was a surprise and also a test of his commitment to the department. He accepted the assignment with an almost convincing smile.

The only other customer eyed him from under a frayed peaked cap. The lack of head on his Guinness suggested it was being nursed carefully. His scruffy, ill matched clothes were in keeping with the fading varnish on the floorboards and the wooden chairs and tables bearing the scars of dragging, banging and no doubt, a few fights.

"You're not from round here?" The observation and question did not require any great deductive skills. In a village of four hundred odd souls there are only those you know and strangers.

"No. I'm from Dublin," he offered cautiously, hoping this would put the other man off the scent.

"A fine city," came the reply. "I was only up there once myself. When Tipperary got to the All-Ireland final and I could afford to go. Them two things haven't happened in a while."

He sipped his pint sparingly, held up the glass for closer inspection of the remaining inch of refreshment and looked pointedly at the stranger.

He was pointedly ignored.

"Have you a name on you?" he continued with the habit of persistence born of desperation.

"I'm Oliver," came the disgruntled reply "and before you ask I'm a geologist and I'm going to be working up on the Knockmealdown mountains for the next few days,"

"I'm Seany," said the new acquaintance sidling himself and his pint down the cigarette marked bar.

"You'd want to be careful on them mountains. There's many a good man never came home from them hills. More than the mist can come down." He dragged the black beer noisily through his yellowing teeth.

"I know my way around mountains, in my line of work," assured Oliver.

"You might know your way around them hills up in Dublin but you don't know your way around these mountains. There's many a story I could tell you that would raise the hair on your neck, if you had the time."

"You and your stories Seany," interjected the barman." He's only here for a week you know, and they will be expecting him to do some bit of work while he's here."

Seany threw a disdainful look over the counter.

"That's the trouble with you young fellas nowadays. Ye know it all. If it's not in a book it doesn't count. Ye would do well to heed the knowledge that's passed down from in here." He jabbed his temple with a nicotine stained forefinger.

Oliver threw the remnants of his pint down his throat and stepped off the stool.

"I've an early start if I'm to get that jeep up that mountain tomorrow." He winked at the barman. "I might see you around before I go back Seany."

"You might," said the crestfallen Seany as the possibility of a free drink edged towards the half open door.

"You mind yourself out there now."

Oliver rose early and had the jeep loaded before breakfast. He ate quickly to escape the grease of his full Irish fry and his landlady's questions as to the nature of his work. He jumped into the cold jeep. It started with a couple of splutters that matched his developing early morning smoker's cough. He crunched it into gear and headed over the small bridge that led onto the mountain road. The twisting road led him through low lying forestry plantations and then onto the Vee where the tapestry of the rich Golden Vale farmland was spread before him. He stopped to look up at Colonel Grubbs grave; a previous landowner who had himself buried with his dog and gun so he could look over his land. A couple of miles later he reached Bay Lough, the glacial lake that was the focus of his work. This small body of water was a leftover of previous global warming, trapped in a valley surrounded by steep wooded peaks and constantly replenished by numerous and never dry mountain streams. The stillness of the air and the dark water was almost palpable. The wind driving the clouds overhead had not reached down this far. He unloaded the jeep, set up his small tent for shelter and laid out his tool belt, rock hammer and pick, sketchpad and pencils. He carefully inspected his compass, magnifiers and pocket transits. When he was satisfied that all the tools of his trade were in order he set to work collecting and labelling samples of rock for later analysis. He worked for two hours and then returned to his tent. As he set his camping stove on a convenient flat rock a movement in the still surround invaded his outer vision.

The woman was bent down at the far side of the lake. He shielded his eyes against the sun. She seemed to be dipping something into the water and then flicking her hand over her shoulder. She seemed unaware of his presence as she continued her rhythmic task. There was something strange about her that he couldn't make out. He looked around to see if anyone else was about. When he turned back the woman had disappeared. He couldn't see where she could have gone so quickly. He was standing on the only track down to the lake. Had he seen shadows thrown by the rhododendron bushes that grew in profusion round the lake?

That bloody Seany, he thought and laughed out loud as he lit the gas stove under the kettle.

That night he slept badly. The image of the woman kept piercing the thin veil of sleep until finally he got up and crept downstairs to find some coffee. His travel clock said five. He gave up any further attempt to sleep. He was intrigued by what he thought he had seen the day before. He was equally intrigued as to why he had dreamt about her.

When he arrived at Bay Lough he walked past his tent to skirt the lake. As he neared the spot where he saw her, his heartbeat seemed to fill his chest. He clambered over the moss covered rocks, excitement mounting, his recent tiredness from his sleepless night overthrown by an expectation, a longing he was at once denying but incapable of suppressing. No sign of her. He turned back, confused by his disappointment. She was standing by a large dolmen type rock less than fifty yards away from where he had come. She was a big woman. He realised that her clothes were the odd thing about her he couldn't explain the previous day. They were long out of fashion. A blue full length skirt billowed out from full hips. A modest white blouse was buttoned to the throat and round her shoulders she held a dark shawl. She reminded him of old postcards he had seen of peasants in their Sunday best. He stood stock still, afraid to move, forcing his eyes not to blink, trying to calm his heart which seemed to be making its way to his throat. He wanted to call out but dared not. She smiled at him from under her jet black hair tied up in a bun and started to dance, slowly at first, her full figure moving with gentle grace. He stood spellbound, drinking in this display that was filling his senses, abandoning any conscious attempt to seek explanation, living totally in the now. She picked up the tempo of the dance to music he could not hear until she was swirling with abandon, her shawl slipping from one shoulder, her breasts straining against the constraints of her blouse and her skirts lifting to reveal glimpses of ankle and calf. She seemed to be laughing, shrieking with the excitement of the dance. But there was no sound. Her bare feet seemed unaffected by the stony dance floor. She slowed and turned towards Oliver, smiled and slipped behind the rock. He started as if in a nightmare and walked on tiptoe to the rock. She was gone.

He slumped to the ground like a boxer who had the breath knocked out of him, holding his shaking head in his hands. He felt an overwhelming sense of loss unlike anything he had felt before. He felt cheated. He was confused. He chided himself. A man of temporal absolutes should not be seeing things. He believed in this world, its origins and evolution. Explanation and seeking explanations were all that could be held to be true. He disdained those who filled the gap in knowledge with superstition, with spirits, with God. These things marked ignorance, science marked enlightenment. But he couldn't dismiss what he had seen and felt and he certainly couldn't explain it.

He abandoned any attempt at work, his tools remained unpacked. He went back to the B&B and spent the rest of the day in fitful sleep. That night he went to the pub early. The owner's wife was behind the bar. Two young lads drinking from bottles barely raised their eyes from the pool game they were playing. Oliver was relieved to see that Seany was at his usual corner spot at the bar.

"Can I buy you a drink Seany?" He pulled up a stool next to him. Seany drained his half full glass with practised ease, wiping the last of the froth across his threadbare jacket.

"Now you're talking the talk. And sure we might as well have something while we are waiting for them to settle." He pointed to the optics set behind the bar.

Oliver ordered whiskey chasers while the half pulled pints of Guinness waited to be brought to black and white perfection.

"Tell me," said Seany eyeing Oliver studiously "What's an educated young man like you doing buying drink for an aul reprobate like me?"

Oliver scanned the small room.

"I was hoping to have a word with you about what you were saying about the mountains, you know, things happening that were hard to explain. I think I've seen something, someone, a woman."

Seany leaned over conspiratorially. "And where did you see this woman?"

"Up at Bay Lough," Oliver whispered aware of some interest being shown by the dumpy woman behind the bar.

Seany placed his glass on the bar. "Oh God between us and all harm." He took off his cap and crossed himself. "What was she doing?"

"The first time I saw her she was bent over at the edge of the lake. The next time she was dancing. Both times she just disappeared. Oh God this sounds so stupid. I must have imagined it. Forget I said anything."

He beckoned with the glass for two more drinks.

"You're not stupid. You've been seeing Petticoat Loose. No doubt about it. Everything fits."

Oliver was angry that his story had not been confirmed by Seany as tricks of the mind.

"Who the hell is Petticoat Loose?"

"Come over here where we can be away from cocked ears and I'll tell you a story." Seany looked pointedly at the barmaid, picked up his drinks and moved to a table at the far corner of the room. Oliver followed meekly.

"Petticoat Loose was a nickname given to a girl named Mary Hannigan who lived not far from here in the early 1800s. Her people were farmers and she was an only child. The story goes that she was a big woman capable of doing a man's work in the fields. She loved dancing and drinking. A bit wild was Mary. The story goes that she married a local boy but at the same time was having an affair with a hedge school master whom she preferred. A year after her wedding her husband disappeared and was never found. The locals believed she had got her lover to do the deed. There were also whisperings that she might be a witch. A year later, at a dance and in the middle of a heavy drinking session Mary, or Petticoat Loose as she known by then dropped dead."

"How did she get the name?"

"God preserve us from the impatience of the young. I'm coming to it." Seany took a healthy swig from his glass.

"One night Mary was at a wedding and was dancing wild, some said like the devil. As she was flying around the floor the buttons of her skirt caught on a nail. Her skirt fell to the ground revealing her petticoats which caused great excitement for those who witnessed it."

Oliver looked unimpressed with the origin of the nickname.

"Where was I?" said Seany.

"Ah yes. For several years after her death nobody mentioned her. Then people started seeing her all over the countryside and she was always creating mischief and frightening people. Now remember she had died without a priest being called; a terrible thing in them days. Eventually people became so frightened they called the priest to get rid of this evil in their midst."

Oliver was silent now, attentive, as Seany slowly unfurled his story.

"The priest deemed her beyond salvation for the murder of her husband. He condemned her to Bay Lough for eternity."

"That's a convenient ending." Oliver's natural scepticism and empiricism resurfaced.

"Don't be such a doubting Thomas," Seany replied "He condemned her to empty the lake with a thimble. That's what you saw when she was bent over near the water."

"Does she appear all the time up there," Oliver enquired more respectfully.

"Only to those she wants to take. When she was alive there were few men could stay with her while she was working, dancing, drinking or God only knows what else. She has her eye on you for sure and you would do well to pack your bags and get the hell away from that place. It is said that the only way she can cross over the bridge between this world and the next and make physical contact is via the water in the lake. Water contains all things to do with this world, old and new. She will tempt you in and then she'll have you like others before you."

Seany stopped talking and walked to the bar with their empty glasses.

Oliver felt elated. He believed his scraggy companion and in that belief he knew, logically, he should have been frightened. But what he felt was the excitement of an expectant lover; the realisation of how he could prevent her disappearing once again filled him with an overwhelming tingling that touched every nerve end. Her dance, her smile, pushed out all other thoughts. He didn't need to know anymore. He only needed to feel like he did now. He gathered his coat from the back of the chair and bolted out the door. He needed to walk, to tire himself out, to make himself sleep, so the morning would come quickly. He strode out of the village, past the old house belonging to long gone landlords, past the two roomed boy's school, and well out past the graveyard with its centuries of stone markers. While his body tired his mind raced in a confusion of thoughts and images that brought tangible pleasure. He barely acknowledged the customary greetings of passers-by.

That night with the aid of the contents of his hip flask he slept well. He woke at six, quietly washing and dressing to escape the inevitable enquiries should he disturb the lady of the house. It was barely seven when he reached the lake. His tools lay undisturbed from the previous day. The frosty air stung his lungs as he reached the lakeside. The white mist was starting to dissipate as the first heat of the sun warmed the earth.

"Mary" he whispered her name. "Mary" he called again, louder this time. His expectation at her coming was tinged with apprehension that she might not appear. There was no sign, no movement round the lake. He took off his trekking boots and thick woollen socks and walked into the water. The pebbles at the edge hurt his feet and the coldness of the water made him stop. Then he saw her. She was standing a few feet away, further into the water, her skirts hiked up above her knees; her right arm extended, her hand open, welcoming. Her smile drew him to her, the cold of the water no longer felt as he placed his hand in hers. She turned and gently led him towards the middle of the lake.

Seany was a little late going to his usual haunt that night. The woman of the house placed a whiskey down for him before he reached his stool.

"It's not like you to be giving free ones," Seany teased. "Where did this come from?"

"You know that Oliver fella. He came back just before we shut last night. He left a drink for you, said he probably wouldn't see you anymore. He said to say thanks."

Seany said nothing. He pulled a wrinkled leather notebook from his jacket pocket. He opened it to a page with a list of names printed in his uneducated scrawl. He removed the short pencil from the spine, licked the tip and wrote "Oliver". He replaced pencil and paper without comment.

"That poor young fellow. We never even got to know his surname," he murmured as he raised the glass to his trembling lips.

Visiting Hours

I think it might be Sunday.

I wouldn't know normally. Everyday merges into every other in this bloody place. I don't count the days anymore. There's nothing to count up to and only one inevitable to count down to. I have stopped naming the days, stopped even the meagre effort of remembering them. I'm like a pagan who has abandoned his gods. No need to remember the Moons day, I don't have to go to work anymore. I'm past useful, past productive. No need to welcome Saturn's day, to spend at home with the family. I've not celebrated this day for a long, long, immeasurable time. In here, we have gone to an earlier, less sophisticated, less confident view of our world where we pray that the setting sun will return once more; heralding one more day's reprieve from our inevitable going.

People come and go in patterns that make no sense to our body clocks. Twenty four hours have been replaced with three time marks, early's, late's and nights, all that is relevant to their time in this place. They arrive before I wake, change when I am at the peak of my day and slip away after I have gone to sleep. Just when I think I have the pattern worked out to some level of predictability they go and change or someone leaves, prompting a reshuffle. In the end I gave up.

They busy themselves in pairs, feeding, washing, turning, straightening. They are mistresses of the non-rhetorical question.

"You'd like a nice bowl of porridge for your breakfast wouldn't you?"

"A nice bed bath and you will look your best won't you?"

I mean where did they get the term bed bath? All it means is that they will either wash you from top to bottom or side to side one bit at a time. I can't remember the last time I was allowed to soak in warm bubbly water, holding my head underneath while I held my nose. There is a bath here with all sorts of hoists and stuff to make it easy on them to get people in and out. The only people who seem to get the benefit are those poor buggers who are doubly incontinent. Soaking in your own shite.

One day when I suggested I had fuck all to look my best for I was visited by the imposing woman in blue who only fills the doorway when doctors and other important people appear. My weekly contribution to her wage packet is obviously not deemed enough to make me important. I try not to abuse this method of summoning the great and the good matron, just enough to keep her on her toes and to allow myself the odd secret smile. In this place any threat to acquiescence is always responded to; just another institution.

They bring me the paper when they are ready, when they have finished with it. They know I like a read. They never bring me the paper I want. The date on the top is only an approximation of what day it actually is. What happens outside this place is only considered important to those who can leave it. It seems I don't need to keep abreast of current affairs. The news is like my mind's wanderings; the past far outweighing in importance the present and future. I have learned slowly, reluctantly, sometimes rebelliously that this is it for me, my final resting place before the final resting place. They never manage to finish the crossword. Too busy or too thick I suppose. I get great pleasure in its completion, folding the paper open on that page so they can see my handiwork.

"Not bad for someone with pre senile dementia." Then one day they stopped commenting. That day I threw the cheap pen they loaned me out the window.

They took away my watch when it rubbed my paper thin skin.

"We don't want your relatives thinking we're not looking after you properly," was the insurance driven explanation as they placed it carefully out of my reach in the bottom drawer of the bedside locker.

That was the last present she bought me for our fiftieth anniversary. She was dead a month later. I had never given a minute's thought to what life without her would be like. I have spent the last five years finding out. Instead of going home after hospital I was moved here for my own safety. I wish they had hopped my head off the wall when they told me. Without her I only have half a life.

Looking at the watch helped me to focus, to remember our time together, and to keep her fresh in this unpredictable failing mind of mine. It was so much easier to remember, to smile, to be warm and wanted when she was still here. Neither of us dreamed that she would go first. All bets were on me, I had been ill for so long. But no, death snatched her that morning when neither of us was looking, another notch on her family tree of weak hearts.

I nearly sure it must be Sunday because I'm wearing my best clothes and I'm out of bed propped on the pee proof chair with sweet smelling pillows. On other days I spend all my time in pyjamas.

"It's handier if you have an accident," I'm offered even though I haven't asked a question.

Handier for you, I mouth silently. It's equally embarrassing for me no matter what clothes I'm wearing. They don't appreciate how being in pyjamas all the time confuses me. I drift off elsewhere and when I drift back to the here and now I'm sometimes not quite sure if I'm waiting to get up or waiting to go to bed. I never wore pyjamas at home. She used to say that no matter how old I got I still have a nice tight bum and there was no need to hide it. The way I am now I'm always waiting for something or waiting for someone before I can do anything.

It must be Sunday.

Your watch is back on my wrist. I don't remember them putting it on. They forgot to wind it and I can't manage it any more with these arthritic fingers. No more accordion playing for me.

It's definitely Sunday.

The family is arranged in the same usual pattern around my room. They always come on a Sunday on their way home from second Mass. It's on their way. The kids are all married, a couple of them more than once. The new grandchildren are brought to me as they appear; a brief pit stop on the way to their inclusive life with the rest of the clan. I've never been to any of their christenings even though one of them is named after me. The female inner circle fusses, replacing old uneaten fruit and old unread magazines with new, rearranging whatever is on the locker, straightening the bed covers and fluffing the recently fluffed pillows. I watch without comment as they inspect their nails and smooth their Sunday best, tossing snippets of conversation back and forth that holds no interest beyond themselves. I keep an eye on the paper for people I know who have died. Unless I bring it up they never mention the latest passing. Do they not know that death is a central part of my present normality, not something to be denied or feared? I realise that only my presence is required at these visitations, my participation is not essential and could, in some ways be hard for them to accommodate. This couple of hours a week is the only overlap I have left with their world and my past.

In the outer circle the men lean on the locker or the windowsill, feet shuffling like they would have at Mass an hour ago and like they will before the match starts in an hour's time. They don't ask me who I think will win anymore. I used to go to all the matches. I'm glad they don't ask me. I don't always know who is playing these days. Working men find it hard to sit and talk in this sort of environment. It never dawns on them that it might be just as hard for me. But to them I am no longer a working man. All them years of doing consigned to my memory and their subconscious. I am merely what they see now. No past. No future. When I catch their eye they smile and nod and toss the odd unconnected comment from their conversation in my general direction. I smile and nod but tend not to answer any more. I fancy I have stopped being their father by blood and law and have become a personification of a future they have every right to fear. It will be easier when I am gone. They can rearrange and select their memories of me. They can find a place in their lives for me that isn't complicated by my present state. They can include me out of kindness, not duty.

In between the adult circles the kids meander in constant motion, stopping only for sweets or whispered admonitions to "be quiet or the nurse will come."

I honestly wish I was dead. Maybe I am. The realization that you won't make any more memories is as near to waking up dead as you can get. I've certainly stopped living. I suppose I will just have to lie here and wait to stop breathing.

We've come a Long Way

The presenter on Lunchtime Choice on the classical radio station Lyric FM, normally so welcoming, so intimate with those making requests, could not hide the surprise in her voice.

"A farmer from County Wexford who is taking a well-earned break from turning the hay in this boiling heat has sent us a text asking us to play some harpsichord music from Bach. Of course we're delighted to (if not a little surprised) so for all those farmers turning the hay here is some Bach."

As he sat in the shade of the idle tractor he heard the slight change in her familiar voice. He knew it well. She was the main reason he listened to classical music again. She had made it re accessible. He tuned in every lunchtime. He often wondered what she was like, what sort of body could hold that breezy bubbly voice , that seeming pleasure felt for complete strangers life events. She would have laughed if she had seen his calloused thumb clumsily tapping out his text message to her. A bit like Bach himself, a lot longer in the composing than the playing.

We've come a long way. The tractors throb was blurred by the earphones transmitting the first bars of his request. Two cars passed silently along the road at the head of the field. No birds interrupted.

He snorted and closed his eyes. His grandfather used to say "We've come a long way" here in this very field as he carried him, his only grandson, shoulder high among the farm labourers and seasonal workers. He never quite knew what his grandfather meant. He just assumed that it was true, judging by the knowing nods and puckered lips of those within earshot. Armed with pitchforks they started after daybreak to toss the hay towards the drying sun, hoping the weather would hold until all the green turned to gold and they could save it into stooks covered with bags and weighted with stones borrowed from the stone walls. They would have no use for his digital watch that left its pale mark on his summer browning and timed his comings and goings.

Sunrise and sunset were the only times that were of importance to them.

He slugged from his sparkling water bottle (he never liked the still) and forked in another mouthful of last night's cold pasta. As his memory wandered to the crisp strains of the harpsichord he could taste again the cold sweet tea that his grandfather used to pass to him.

"Drinking with the big men." He tousled his hair making him feel six feet tall. He could feel again the tightness of his lips as he made sure the paper twist cork was tight to prevent any spillage. He had the job of standing them in the stream to keep them cool and to fill empty bottles with the cold water from under the small weir. Today the stream behind the ditch tinkled its light sparkles onwards undisturbed by his thirst.

We've certainly come a long way he thought as he replaced his drink into the cooler box.

He shifted the sunglasses that had slipped on the sweat on his nose. His grandfather used to lift the frayed peak of his cap and then flick his tongue from one side of his mouth to the other (always left to right) to gather the salty rivulets of exertion. A scratch of his head, a repositioning of the cap, an eye to the sky to gauge the weather and then back to the rhythmic toil. The weather always had more than its fair share of the conversation that came and went on the soft breeze between the workers. Each had his own favourite sign for predicting good weather, be it the cuckoo calling in a clear voice , or frogs and tadpoles seen in the middle of a pond or mist clearing from the nearby hills in the early morning, each trying to maintain an optimism about this important annual event. No one would be paid until the hay was saved. He hadn't thought about those signs for many a long year. He wondered how many he had forgotten since he placed his faith in the 5 day forecast on teletext.

The music stopped cleanly, leaving a few moments of utter silence before she reminded everyone again about the farmer from Wexford saving hay. The silence startled him as, in his reverie, he was waiting to hear the abrasive crackle as the needle ran off to the edge of his grandmother's treasured records and her bustle as she lifted the needle gently with her usual acclamation to no one in particular of "Wasn't that just lovely". She always wiped them front and back with a black square of muslin kept near her small stack before sliding them reverentially into their yellowing covers and replacing them in the sideboard in the small parlour. She played them after Sunday tea when her apron was hung up behind the kitchen door. Her favourite was the harpsichord by Bach.

"Music good enough for heaven and earth," she used to tell him as he crept quietly in to sit beside her.

His grandfather dismissed the music as for those with notions. He tried to coax a more modern signal from the brown wireless in the back room.

He stirred, pulling the earphones free, stretching himself back into the cab. The tractor started at the first turn of the key, vibrating under his cushioned seat, the clackety clack of the hay turning machine hung behind filling all the space around and above him. He looked round the empty field and onwards to the empty house that had come to him early when tuberculosis stopped his father breathing this same air. He had left school then to look after his mother and the farm. She had faded away before his inattentive eyes, never quite the same , content only to wait and see her only child settled into manhood, seeing no further reason to stay. No other woman had come to take her place.

Now he was alone, getting pleasure from the warmth in a strangers voice every lunchtime.

"We've come a long way alright," he muttered "from pastoral symphony to one man band."

The tractor shunted forward on its predictable round. On Lyric FM someone else's moment was announced with enthusiasm.